PRECIOUS RASCAL
By Larry Incollingo
Copyright, 1994
A Reunion Series Book

Published by Reunion Books
3949 Old SR 446
Bloomington, IN 47401

Other Books By Larry Incollingo
Laughing All The Way
G'bye My Honey
Ol' Sam Payton

*See order coupon in back of book to obtain or
reserve copies of these books.*

ACKNOWLEDGEMENT

For their help and cooperation I am deeply indebted to Scott C. Schurz, Publisher of the Bloomington, Indiana, *Herald-Times* and Bloomington and Bedford *Sunday Herald-Times* and the Bedford, Indiana, *Times Mail*, and Mike Hefron, General Manager of the *Herald-Times*, and Bill Schrader, Editor and General Manager of the *Times-Mail*. LInc.

For my grandchildren.

THE COVER

The cover and illustrations for *Precious Rascal*, as well as the covers for its companion books *G'bye My Honey*, and *Ol' Sam Payton*, and for my book *Laughing All The Way*, are the creations of my gifted son-in-law, Gerald Strange. Gerald is a native of Burns City, in Martin County, Indiana, and is employed at the Naval Surface Warfare Center, Crane. He is available for and welcomes illustrating opportunities. Affectionately known as "Mouse," a caricature of a mouse appears as a tag in all his work.

A Word About
PRECIOUS RASCAL
Book 2
Of The Reunion Series

Precious Rascal is a continuation of *G'bye My Honey*," the first of the Reunion Series.

Contents come from the same source – more than a quarter century of traveling and talking with Hoosiers in southern Indiana for my newspapers, the *Herald-Times* and the *Sunday Herald-Times* in Bloomington, and the *Daily Times-Mail*, in Bedford, Indiana.

As in *G'bye My Honey*, the characters who brighten these pages are also just people like you and your friends, perhaps like your father or mother, an uncle or aunt, a co-worker, or one or more of your neighbors.

You will find heroes here, too, but you won't find anyone famous or anyone rich. Simply put, these people were chosen because of the amusement, pleasure, courage, faith and understanding that they have brought to the lives of countless others, and especially to me.

I sincerely hope you enjoy reading *Precious Rascal* and that you will look forward to *Ol' Sam Payton*, the third book of the Reunion Series, to be published soon. LInc.

THANKSGIVING

Should you drive north on the narrow blacktop that runs along the railroad tracks through Stinesville, and turn and jog where you're supposed to, you'll soon come to where Emery Crissmore used to live. The old house sits on a hill, overlooking a bend of the West Fork of the White River. When Emery lived there, and he'd hear you coming, he'd step out to meet and greet you. If he didn't hear you, and he didn't step outside to prevent it, his dogs might have feasted on you.

"A dog never did bite anyone who is not going to harm you," Emery said to ease my concern on that mid-November day. His dogs sent me a different message. Emery then went on to emphasize the very excellent possibility that his dogs might attack some people. I got the impression he wasn't sure of what his dogs might or might not do.

Emery had lived alone on that hill ever since the death of his wife, two years before my visit. He got so lonely sometimes that he'd have given almost anything to have had someone to visit with. One day while he was at the grocery store down in town, he told the usual bunch of loungers there, "Boys, there's

1

times when I get so lonely that I think I'll just put a sign down by the road and offer seventy-five cents an hour to anybody who'll come up and talk to me."

Considering Emery's financial status, seventy-five cents an hour represented a lot of L-O-N-E-L-Y. He didn't have that kind of money. Neither did he have any rich relatives he could depend on to die and leave him a bundle. "There never even were any rich neighbors around here," he told me during my visit. He ought to have known. He was eighty-one past, as he put it, and he was born and raised on that hill, married there, and celebrated all the Thanksgiving Days of his life there. Thanksgiving was the purpose of my visit, to learn how a man alone, as he was, would spend the coming holiday. He preferred to talk about Thanksgivings past.

"We raised hogs and we made lots of sausage and canned it," he said. "But Thanksgiving? Really, it wasn't ever too much. We'd just call it a family time."

What a family it was. Seven boys and one girl, and a father and a mother. "We'd generally always have a turkey," he said. "We raised them, see? And we'd just kill one. I remember one Thanksgiving we killed a big fat goose. But I didn't like that as well as turkey. Seems like it was all fat and grease."

There was a benevolence in the manner of Emery's narration that seemed to leave me breathlessly swept up into his deepest confidence, that I was privileged to share in something treasured and of great value. I hung on every word as though I had missed the best of joys as he continued, "We always put up walnuts, and on Thanksgiving we'd crack them and pop a dishpan full of popcorn. And we'd make popcorn balls and pour syrup over them – generally sorghum, with sugar added. Talk about good. I never will forget, one of my brothers always went for the biggest popcorn

2

ball, and one time my mother and sister made one around a big cold biscuit. Oh, he got a surprise all right, when he got that one." Emery laughed heartily at the memory.

Older persons who still live in a house as Emery did, who are still surrounded by good memories, as Emery was, and who are still dependent on no one but themselves, as Emery was, seem to have a spirit of laughter about them that so many older folks in different living situations don't have. Older folks who live in a house as Emery did, also cry. Just like everyone else, they have their reasons for both. Emery fought back some tears as he told me about his son, Basil, who lived in Illinois and had undergone surgery for a tumor on the brain and was not doing well. He presently returned his thoughts to Thanksgiving. "My mother always fixed a dinner for the poor, or older folks," he remembered. "And it always fell to me to take it to them."

Something he didn't say about that struck him funny and he laughed again, his blue eyes sparkling behind aging gold frames. Whatever it was, he chose not to share it. His head, on which a leather cap was tilted at just the right angle for an octogenarian, bobbed up and down with his continued pleasure. Sometimes when he laughed he passed the palms of his hands in a forward motion over his corduroy pants, where they showed wear above his knees. I got the impression that in his way he was perhaps savoring again a happy, private memory. Perhaps he was just rubbing the warmth from his wood stove into his bony thighs. I didn't ask, or pry. But older folks will do that, too, you know, rub the heat from a stove into their thighs or backsides.

"Never ate beans at Thanksgiving," Emery continued laughing and rubbing his thighs. "We had to pick

3

them. Oooo! That was work. Then we'd have to hull them, put them in a bed sheet and take them to the hayloft, where we'd have to beat them around. They were a lot of work, and I don't like them for that reason, still today."

Emery was silent for a time. When he spoke again his words seemed to come from a distance. "I remember one Thanksgiving – first year we were married; 1913. Ruby and I went to a shooting match a mile west of town, on Wolf Mountain. It was a nice warm day. I remember we wore sweaters, and had to take them off. I won a turkey, and we'd already had dinner. But, oh, we had such a good time that day."

MAILBOX RENDEZVOUS

In some ways it may have been a better time to have lived, when Idas Armstrong was a girl growing up on a farm between Bloomington and Bedford. She believed as much, anyway, even after decades of change – as it is often argued – for the better.

There were Idas, her sister, Ora, and their brothers, Ray, Evan and Ellis, and almost four hundred rolling acres on which they were reared. Grant Armstrong and his three sons worked with cattle, hogs and sheep. The girls aided their mother, Emma Whisenand Armstrong, with the cooking, the housework, the canning, and with the chickens and the eggs. They also learned to tat.

Eventually, there was for Idas, too, the rural mail carrier, a youth named Robert Roland Ellison. When he appeared in his buggy, she'd make some excuse to meet him at the roadside mailbox. Ultimately, they would marry – in Springville – and in later years they would, with their daughter and son-in-law, operate a hardware store in Bedford.

"In a way it was a better time to live," Idas Armstrong Ellison said at the beginning of our visit in her home at 1428 Thirteenth St., in Bedford. "Life is too

5

fast now, for one thing. And although there are more advantages now, I think our time, living on a farm, was better. My father was not rich, like some. But usually he had two or three hundred head of cattle and a big lot of hogs and sheep, and was able to care for his own. There was no work for us girls, only cooking and the like. We learned to cook when we were so small we had to stand on a box to reach the cook table. We had nothing but happiness back then."

There were the chickens and the eggs from which the girls earned money. Tatting brought them more money.

"We made a lot of tatting," she said. "We did tablecloths, sheets and pillow cases and all kinds of fancy things. A pair of pillow cases and sheets would bring eighteen dollars, and as much as twenty-five. When we weren't cooking or keeping house, we were tatting. We tatted all the time. We could just go like lightning with it."

When she and her sister, Ora, got in the notion for a new car, they gave their father five hundred dollars of their own earned cash and asked him to go to Bedford and buy them one. Grant returned that afternoon with a new Model-T Ford with side curtains.

"A man drove it home, and our dad came home with him," she recalled the event. "You didn't have to have a driver's license back then, just get in and drive. And we did." After a pause, during which she seemed to be luxuriating in the memory, she continued, "I can't remember that anyone ever taught us to drive. We had plenty of space to practice, and we just climbed into the car and practiced." She laughed quietly as though reviewing in her mind some humorous recollection of that time – which she did not reveal to me – until she was ready to dismiss it, then said, "It was a brand new car, right out of the factory. And when it rained we put the side curtains up."

By then another new Model-T had appeared in the neighborhood. The mail carrier's. Actually, it was his father's. Fathers laid claim to everything in the family in those days, and Idas's and Ora's car had its claimant in Grant. But claims notwithstanding, Model-Ts were faster, more comfortable than buggies, and the mail carrier knew it. He was also aware that the Model-T would get him to Idas's house not only faster and in more comfort than a buggy, but also in style.

I liked the looks of Roland from the first time that I saw him," Idas remembered her initial feelings for the young mail carrier. "I'd see him coming out the road and I'd go out to get the mail. He'd be waiting for me. And when I'd get to the mailbox we'd talk and joke and laugh."

They talked and joked and laughed at the roadside mailbox for three years. Then, in a more serious vein one day, they climbed into the young mail carrier's Model-T and drove to Springville, home to the Armstrong clan, where in a simple ceremony Reverend Quincy Short pronounced them man and wife.

"My father and his brothers were all born at Springville, where Uncle Curtis Armstrong lived, and we always called Springville our home," she explained the choice of the wedding site. "Quincy's father married my grandfather and grandmother, so we had Quincy marry us."

It was years later that they and their daughter, Mildred, and her husband, Robert (Bob) Szatowski, bought out Heitger's Hardware Store, on the east side of the Courthouse Square, in Bedford. The establishment became known as Ellison's Hardware, and a first-time shopper in the friendly place knew almost immediately that it was a family owned store.

In subsequent years, the Ellisons enjoyed many successes there. Then Roland fell ill and died. Alone

7

then, Idas asked Bob and Mildred to move into her home with her. Then Bob passed away.

In the cool quiet of Idas's lovely home, it became again hard to believe that time in its passage can be so abrasive. But it was a short-lived thought for Idas's voice interrupted. When I looked up she was smiling. "I do declare, it was better living back then," she was saying. "But I've always enjoyed my life. I still am enjoying it. And I just want to keep on and keep on and keep on."

In spite of Grant Armstrong claiming the Model-T after she and Roland were married, Idas, who was on the brink of her 90th birthday at the time of my visit in 1981, expressed no regrets about the past.

THE TOTEM POLE

During a period when the late Tom Lemon was mayor of Bloomington, the color lemon yellow decorated many city properties, including its police cruisers.

One night, while gloriously besotted with spirits, Jim Ayers, who now is also with the saints, staggered out of a city tavern. Thinking he was getting into a Yellow Cab, he mistakenly climbed into a yellow police car. Promptly taken to the county jail, he was booked as a drunk, and locked up.

Next morning, there was joy in the jail. Jim, a regular visitor there, was a fine cook, and the jail just happened to be in dire need of one. Sobered, showered, shaking, he was dutifully at work in the jail's kitchen.

"When they'd run out of a cook down at the jail, they'd come looking for Jim and arrest him," a bartender in a city tavern remembered. "He was usually drunk and they'd get him for public intoxication."

"Old Jim made the best brain sandwiches you ever tasted," devoted friend, Bob Nellis, said, remembering the days when Jim cooked at Skinner's Cafe on N. College Avenue.

"Nobody could make chili like Jim," Butch Gastineau's wife, Ann, was known to say. She used to have someone go into Skinner's for take-outs for her.

"That was back when it was against the law for women to sit at the bar," another of Jim's old friends, Bill Harris, said. He pinpointed the time as that era when a respectable housewife wouldn't be caught dead in a drinking establishment, when Kenneth "Skinner" Rush and his wife, Thelma, owned the cafe. "You never saw women in the place," he said.

Besides being a good cook, "When he was sober, Jim could paint you a sign as good as any sign painter," Bill added. "He'd ask you for money to buy paint for your sign and then go right to a tavern and drink it up. Then he'd come back and tell you he needed more money to buy paint. Hell of it was, painted signs went out of style before he could get sober.

"He'd sober up once in a while," Bill said. After a moment's thought he added, "He was a good boy, Jim was. He wasn't a drunk. He was like me and a lot of other people, he just couldn't stay sober."

Whatever he was, Jim is remembered by those who knew him best as a good guy, one who could sit next to someone's hamburger on the bar and never steal it. And he'd buy anybody a beer who walked in the door, if he had the money.

A veteran, Jim rarely spoke of his World War II experiences. "When me and him was together, he'd tell me lots of things," Bill remembered. "But Jim was drunk and I was drunk and I don't remember anything he told me."

Jim received a soldier's pension from the government. Nothing like what a congressman would get. From that and his meager earnings, he retained an attorney. "Had him on his payroll," is the way Bob Nellis put it. "For twenty-five dollars he'd either get

Jim out of jail or keep him from going back, whatever his predicament at the time."

Because he needed a place to stay one winter, Jim lived at Bob's remote country place. It was a campground named Bob's Five Little Acres, south of Lake Monroe, and he paid for his keep by doing odd jobs there. Although it was about eleven miles from the nearest tavern, and Jim didn't drive, he seemed content to live in the house while Bob stayed in town. They had been friends for many years and often fished and camped together, and Bob trusted him implicitly.

Jim triumphed over the lonely separation from town that winter in two remarkably memorable ways. He secretly guzzled a cache of Bob's whiskey in such a clever manner that Bob did not learn of his loss until months later.

"He drank most of the whiskey from each bottle, refilled them with water, and reglued the cap seals," Bob said. "Out of seventy-five bottles I had stashed there, he left me about two gallons of watered-down whiskey."

Jim's other accomplishment was less evasive. He cut down a tree and when he wasn't drinking or watering down Bob's whiskey, he carved it into a totem pole as a gift for his benefactor. Touched, Bob helped him prepare a concrete base and together they stood the symbolic shaft on it at Jim's own choice of location, the entrance to the campground.

Jim had a stomach ailment he ignored until it got him down. A dear friend, "Boodles" Chitwood, who owned a downtown tavern, arranged his admission to a veterans' hospital. By then Jim was living in government subsidized housing and Boodles went there and made him go to the hospital. She liked Jim, and it was a motherly, loving effort on her part.

11

But Jim had drunk too much whiskey in his lifetime, and he didn't last long after that. Boodles went to his wake at a city funeral home and was impressed by what she saw. It was replete with organ music and mourners, some being Jim's old friends, and a few older ladies from the government subsidized housing complex, which was Jim's last address in this life.

After the service Jim was cremated. His ashes waited in a cardboard box at the mortuary for someone to claim them. He had relatives; someone thought a sister, a half-brother, maybe two. No one was sure anymore. But for months there were no takers. In the end his good friend Bob claimed what was left of his old fishing companion. "I put him on the passenger seat beside me in my pickup," Bob said, "and we drove out to the camp. When we got there, I put him on a shelf in the kitchen."

Jim's altered presence posed no problem, except that Bob felt that his friend should have a proper burial. "And everyday," Bob recalled, "I'd look up at him and say, 'Jim, where do you think I ought to bury you?' "

That's the way it was for months; Bob asking and Jim not answering. "One day I thought I'd put him in the pond back of the house because we had fished so much together. Then I said, 'No, Jim. In winter you'd freeze in that cold water.' Then one day I told him, 'Jim, I think I'll put you in the ground where you belong.' "

When the time was right, Bob took up a posthole digger, put Jim under his arm, and carried them both to where he and Jim so many years earlier had installed the totem pole.

"This," Bob told his friend as he started digging near the base of the emotionless wooden faces, "is where I'm going to put you, Jim. This is where you belong."

And there, while we stood contemplating a tiny metal marker bearing the appropriate legend at the base of that decaying, crumbling, upright wooden shaft, Bob held, for my sake, one sunny morning, an ad hoc get-acquainted memorial service for his old fishing buddy, one James Ayers, 1914-1984.

AUNT GERTIE

One of the more devastating floods in American history took place in Ohio and Indiana in 1913. Seventy-seven people in Indiana were killed. The main cause of that disaster was torrential rains that dumped ten times more water into the Miami River than it could hold. But in a one-time Republican stronghold now covered by the waters of Lake Monroe, the people blamed that flood on the Virginia-born son of a Presbyterian minister.

"We called it 'the Wilson flood,' " Aunt Gertie Henry told me during my visit with her one afternoon.

Woodrow Wilson, former managing editor of the Princeton University *Princetonian*, former lawyer and Princeton University president, and governor of New Jersey, was elected twenty-eighth President of the United States the previous November. Soon after his inauguration in March, the flood of 1913 inundated the land.

"And we were in it," Aunt Gertie said, "and I've been wanting to tell you about it. We's all Republicans, there where we lived by the old Cutright covered bridge. And when the flood come along, Wilson hadn't been in office too long, so we named it after him. Because he was a Democrat, of course."

Aunt Gertie was born, raised, married and lived on Cutright Hill, above the bridge. Her brother, Jim, lived down in the bottoms, on the banks of Salt Creek. A second brother, Don, also lived nearby, but away from the creekbed.

"It commenced t'rainin' and stormin' the night before," Aunt Gertie recounted from memory an ordeal that would last eleven hours. "Now that was a rain, believe me. We thought it would never stop. And the wind just raged, and it rolled the metal roof right off'n the kitchen and blew it away. Next mornin' I had to ladle water out of the cookstove before I could get a fire built to fix something to eat."

Long before she began ladling water out of the stove, however, her brother, Jim, had awakened about four a.m. and, realizing that his family was in danger, alerted his wife, Anna, to the rising creek waters.

"He told her t'fix some breakfast and then they'd get out of there," Aunt Gertie continued. "But before they could do that the water was up in the house. They put the children on the bed, Anna got in the washing tub, and Jim put on his hip boots and went out and started hollerin' to the hill."

Joshua Waldrip, his wife, Serepta (Aunt Rep), and Gertie's brother, Don, and his wife and family, and Aunt Gertie, then twenty-two, and her husband, all could hear Jim calling for help.

"But when we'd call back to him he couldn't hear us," Aunt Gertie said. "And we knew that him and his family was in grave danger."

Joshua and his son then began caulking an old boat, preparing it for a rescue mission. By that time Aunt Gertie, with the help of some other women from the rural neighborhood who had congregated at her house, had cleaned the wet ashes from the fireplace and bailed out the stove. They soon had crackling fires burning in both, and had breakfast "acookin' " for Don's kids.

"Everybody had a woodshed then, and we had ours, and there was plenty of dry wood for fires," Aunt Gertie said.

Meanwhile, Joshua and Don had rowed across the racing, high waters and returned safely with three of Jim's four children. They then again pitted their strength and daring against the rising flood to return to Jim's home. Arriving there safely they helped Anna and the baby to the barn loft for temporary safety. They also took time to throw down enough hay to build a ramp, up which they drove two horses and three head of cattle, securing them in the loft apart from Anna and her child. The three men then spread hay in the lofts of a double corn crib, and into the safety of them they lifted hogs and chickens. A contrary rooster, squawking hysterically and madly flapping its wings, escaped, flying free of their good intentions. Alas, the angry bird's ability to fly was limited and it was unable to reach land. Exhausted, finally, it glided to a forced landing in the surging water and drowned.

The men's efforts took up valuable time. It was three o'clock in the afternoon before they brought Anna and the baby down from the barn loft and were ready to challenge the flood again. The small boat, its gunwales nearly underwater from the combined weight of Joshua, Don, Jim, and Anna and her child, was pushed out into the flood.

"By that time the water was really high and it was runnin' swift," Aunt Gertie remembered the hazards of that trip. "The men couldn't row straight across.

They had to go with the current. Once, when they disappeared behind some trees, we thought they was lost. But they wasn't. We saw them again and we was glad. We clapped and we hollered. And they got to the hill all right."

Aunt Gertie had waited a long time to recount this experience. She was in her mid-eighties at the time and, having left Cutright Hill just prior to the construction of Lake Monroe, was sharing a home in Bloomington with Virginia Vaughn. She was the oldest active member of the Burgoon Baptist Church, where she was baptized July 21, 1907. As a girl she attended a one-room school that stood near the church.

"That's where I l'arnt what all I l'arnt," she told me, her eyes a-twinkle. "Ray Lampkin was a teacher, so's Elmer Ferguson. And Cora McCormick, Jason Browning, Riley Butcher, Tighe Hays, Cap Hays and Logan Browning was all classmates of mine."

Aunt Gertie had no children of her own. Jim had four, Don had ten, and her sister, Molly Sexton, had eleven. "I baby-setted with all of them and I sewed for all of them," she began a rush of words that left her almost breathless. "I remember one time one of them had 'hoopin' cough and was black in the face chokin', time I got there. And they's pitchin' her up in the air, and her mother was alayin' in the kitchen floor fainted, like she was dead. And I retched my finger down that child's throat and I pulled out the biggest bunch of phlegm out o'her. And she's alive today."

Recalling that the years living amid the rest of the Republicans on Cutright Hill were good ones, Aunt Gertie pointed out that, "We was all peaceful."

A faithful member of Burgoon Baptist Church for her entire life, she was equally faithful to the Republican Party except for the last election. Voting an absentee ballot, which was not unusual for rural residents without means of reaching the polls on election day, Aunt Gertie inadvertently X-ed the wrong square and voted a straight Democrat ticket.

"I voted in the wrong place but I didn't lose my vote," she philosophically reviewed the error. "I aimed to vote'r straight, and I did. But I felt guilty. I felt like I hadn't ought to've done it."

Eddie Crum - The Early Years

PRECIOUS RASCAL

The blue in Eddie Crum's eyes was faded from eighty-five years of viewing life, and his proportionately small shoulders were stooped from the living of it. He had unusually large ears for a small man, and the thick mass of hair on his head belied his days, for it was black, showing only touches of gray.

But singing and strumming a guitar or banjo, and fiddling such tunes as "Maid In The Garden Sifting Sand," or "Eight More Miles to Louisville," or his own "Midnight Eddie," or his "Burglar Song," Eddie would double in size, he was that good a musician and entertainer. And, as such, he was as refreshing as a cooling · summer evening breeze.

Eddie always said that his musical talent went back to his mother, who was a natural born musician. "And," he observed one day, "I never had a lesson in my life, I got it from her, and our five kids get it from me. They all play, and, if you'll come over some Sunday evening, you can hear us. We always have a round on Sunday evening."

Eddie stopped talking long enough that day to strum his guitar and sing a few songs. When he had satisfied himself he paused to recall an early family event. "We were the first family to play and sing over old WLAP, in Louisville, Kentucky," he said. "Me and the old woman and the five kids. But that's the short story of it. While we were there one of the kids took the measles. We were supposed to be quarantined. But I only had seventeen dollars, and the man from the Board of Health said, 'If you go straight home and not let anyone out of the car, I'll let you go.' Now that's just the case, exactly. It just gave me the blues so bad I just never did go back to sing on the radio."

Eddie's son, Festus, who was a member of the troupe that made the jaunt to Louisville, remembered the event differently. "Mom didn't go to Louisville," he said at the time of this writing. In his seventies at this time, Festus said he was ten or eleven when he, his brothers, Clayton and Edward, and their sister, Forrest, accompanied their father to Louisville to audition at WLAP.

"The man did like us and he said he would put us on the air in the morning. But Dad wouldn't stay

20

overnight. He was one of those kind of people who liked to be home at nighttime and he told the man, 'I wouldn't stay all night in Louisville if you gave me the place.' And we came home. No one had the measles, either," Festus continued. "I don't know where that part of the story came from. I suppose Dad might have just told it one time and then got to believing it."

Eddie Crum - The Later Years

If the blues still remained with Eddie when we visited he kept them well hidden. His conversation was light, animated, and he appeared pleased and happy. The small house that was his home in rural Harrodsburg, some dozen miles or more south of Bloomington, was aglow with him, his words, his songs. The "old woman" to whom he referred was his lovely wife, Edna McNeely Crum, a tiny, white-haired lady "No bigger," as Eddie put it, "than a pound of soap," who shared the home with him. She also was a musician, having played the piano in her youth.

"I used to visit here," she said of earlier days when she traveled from her home at Ellettsville to Harrodsburg, where Eddie was reared and where he had lived all his life. "He used to call me 'Mousey' because I was so small," Edna said. "Oh, he used to make me so mad. And he wouldn't stop calling me that. He wouldn't stop on nothing."

She looked back on sixty-one years of marriage to Eddie, and she vowed that the association had wrought no change in him. She declared that given the opportunity she would not marry him again. Nor would she marry any man, for that matter, she hurried to add. As she spoke, she defiantly shook her small white head. Still, she had married Eddie, and she admitted she was satisfied with that. But marrying him wasn't the easiest thing she'd ever done. It took some doing – two trips to the preacher's house before that man of divine calling succeeded in joining them as man and wife.

"The first time," Eddie began recounting the two occasions with eyes alight, "the preacher asked me, 'Do you take this woman to be your lawful wedded wife?' And I said, 'Yes sir.' And he said to her, 'Do you take this man to be your lawful wedded husband?' She didn't say anything. I looked over at her and she had fainted."

Both laughed then, Eddie more than Edna, and, when he had laughed enough, he resumed his story. "So, I took her home," he said. "And I fed her some vitamins, and, when she was strong enough, I took her back to that preacher. And I told him, 'Now Preacher,' I said, 'Don't ask any more of those damn-fool questions. Just tie the knot and get it over with.' "

The marriage ended an on-again off-again romance Eddie was having with a girl named Sally Skinner. In those early days in rural Monroe County young and old folks alike derived much of their social entertainment from attending Sunday and week-night church services. So that they might be together, Eddie and Sally had attended their share. At one of them they became separated. Eddie recalled the incident in this manner: "They were all asingin' and ajumpin', and I was alookin' for my girl. I bumped into the preacher. He looked at me and said, 'Son, are you alookin' for sal-a-vation?' I looked right back at him and I said, 'No, Preacher, I'm alookin' for Sa-l-l-y Skinner.'

"When I first started goin' with Sally," he went on, "I asked my mother one night what I ought to say to her when I went to her house. My mother said, 'Son, just say somethin' soft.' When Sally answered my knock on her door and said, "Why how-do-you-do–' " Eddie had raised his voice to a falsetto to affect the sound of a woman's voice "– I said, 'Mashed potatoes,' which was about the softest thing I could think of right then."

Although he had been to Louisville, Eddie had never seen Indianapolis. A homebody, travel seemed of little importance to him. He enjoyed life in Harrodsburg and seemed very happy being there. He traveled only to where his job as a house painter took him, and where his music might take him. He was a good house painter, and he was able to earn a livelihood in that line of work.

Festus remembered a story Eddie used to tell when asked how he became a house painter. "Dad and 'Herk' Hazel worked at Claude Smallwood's General Store in Harrodsburg," he recounted the tale. "One day a lady came in to buy some hose, but she didn't know exactly what size she wore. So Claude gave her a pair of stockings and said, 'You take these into that side room. There's a chair in there. You sit down and try them on and see if they fit all right.' Then he turned to Dad and Herk and he said, 'And if I catch either one of you peeping in there you'll be fired.' And then Dad would say, " 'After I lost that job I went to painting houses.' "

Although he was a good house painter, Eddie Crum was best known, and loved, for his music, and appreciated for his unpredictable sense of humor. The memorable dead fish caper was one of his pranks. After someone had given him an enormous dead carp, he attached it to the line of a fishing pole and sat angler-like on a concrete abutment over a dry ditch at the Harrodsburg turn-off and State Road 37, across from Fowler's Garage. Each time a car approached on the highway, Eddie gave a yank on the pole, flipping the big fish up in the air where it appeared to be very much alive and struggling to unhook itself. To passing motorists, it was a stunning, if incredulous, sight. Eyes popping in surprise, some drivers even whipped their heads around for a second look, nearly running their cars off the road. After a few near accidents, Eddie wisely quit the little game.

When she learned of that prank, Edna shook her head in dismay and exclaimed, "He gets worse all the time." Which is what Jenny Tillie must have thought. Miss Tillie taught school at Harrodsburg when Eddie was a boy. "She asked me to recite somethin' one day, and I didn't want to recite nothin'," Eddie recalled during our visit. "And she forced me. So I said, 'Jack and Jill went up the hill, to fetch a pail of water. Jack fell down and broke a ten-dollar bill, and Jill picked up a dollar and a quarter.' Miss Tillie got awfully mad, and she said, 'I'll tend to you after school, young man.' And she did."

He paused a moment, then added, "A dollar and a quarter is what the preacher got for marrying us. After he tied the knot I said, 'Preacher what does the law allow you for a marriage?' And he said, 'One dollar.' So I gave him a quarter and I said, 'Here, this'll make you a dollar and a quarter.' "

Six children were born of Edna's marriage to Eddie, one of whom died in infancy. At this writing, the remaining five were still living in the Harrodsburg-Bloomington area. They are Clayton, Festus, Edward, Forrest and Phyllis.

"One doctor delivered all of the kids but me," Forrest said during a visit with her some years after the loss of her parents. "The one who delivered me had served in France during World War I, and I was supposed to have been named after a sweetheart he left over there. Somehow the name turned out to be Forrest, and I've had problems galore with it ever since." Then displaying a characteristic typical of her father, she added, "One time I was admitted to the hospital and I was given a bed in a men's ward. Of course I said, 'Hey, I'll stay!' I saw nothing wrong with that arrangement. But they wouldn't let me. But you wouldn't believe the trouble I've had with that name."

Forrest remembered that her father was something of an insomniac, and to while away sleepless hours he would turn to music. "He'd get up and take a banjo, fiddle or guitar down from the wall where he kept them hanging, and he'd play," she said. "Many were the times I woke up in the night and heard him just playing away."

Eddie had a collection of songs he could call to mind as easily as he could the time of day. One of his favorites was "The Burglar Song," a tune he wrote and once presented at a command performance one afternoon before Judge Nat U. Hill and office workers in the circuit court room of the Monroe County Court House, in Bloomington. The lyrics, which brought laughter and applause from Eddie's listeners went something like this:

I'll sing you a song of a burglar, who went to rob a
    house.
He come in at the window, he come quiet as a
    mouse.
Under the bed this burglar went, his face ag'in
    the wall.
He didn't know it was an old maid's house,
Or he wouldn't have had the gall.

He thought about all the things he would get
While under the bed he lay,
But at nine o'clock he saw a sight
That turned his whiskers gray.

The old maid came in at that hour of nine,
"Oh, I'm so tired," she said.
Thinkin' everything was all right
She didn't look under the bed.

She took out her teeth and a bum glass eye,
And a wig from off'n her head;
And the burglar had forty-nine fits
When he looked out from under the bed.

He never said nothin', nary a word,
He was quiet as a clam.
She said, "Thank God my prayer's answered,
I think I got me a man."

The burglar came out from under the bed,
His face a total wreck.
The old maid bein' wide awake,
She grabbed him around the neck.

She stuck a revolver in his face,
And to this burglar she said,

"Young man, you'll marry me
Or I'll blow off the top of your head."

The burglar looked around the room,
He saw no place to scoot.
He looked at her teeth and her bum glass eye,
And he said, "For God's sake, SHOOT!"

"He wanted all of us kids to play music, too," Forrest resumed the memory of her father. "And he had a special way of getting us interested. When he left the house in the morning he would tell my mother loud enough for all of us to hear, 'Don't let those kids touch a damn one of those instruments while I'm gone.' Since we were forbidden to touch them, we naturally did, and we learned to play."

There came a time when Forrest would go far beyond what Eddie expected of his children. She had been pestering her father to buy her a bicycle. Unconvinced that she needed one, he more or less ignored her. "Well, one day," Forrest recounted, "I guess I was thirteen, here come Sam Chambers, riding his bike, and I called out to him. I said, 'Hey! How would you like to trade that bike for a good guitar?' Sam said, 'I don't know. Let's see it.' So I took him into the house and showed him Dad's guitar, where it hung on the wall. I said, 'How about that one?' And we traded. When Dad found out I got a licking. Did I ever get a licking!"

The bike was much too large for Forrest, "Or," as she recalled, "I was too little for it." Still, she persisted in trying to ride it. One day while she was thus occupied, and the bike had a flat tire, she got into a wreck and suffered a number of injuries. Eddie, fearing for her future safety, and probably still angry that she had traded his guitar for a troublesome bicycle, took an axe to the two-wheeled vehicle.

27

"He just chopped it up in pieces," Forrest said.

There were other sides to Eddie and still another of them was revealed by his son, Festus. "My dad was a man who didn't covet another man's possessions," he recalled. "It wouldn't bother him a bit that one of his neighbors might have a big, fine automobile. My dad would be satisfied with a horse and buggy, and he'd never say a word about what the other fellow might have. He lived his own life, and he didn't try to run the other fellow's business. Mom was the same way," he said.

Festus remembered that his father did have an automobile in the early days. "I think it was a 1923 model touring car that he might have driven sometimes. But Dad wasn't a driver. I remember that in 1930 I worked a hundred days for Wyatt Fowler for a Model-T Ford. A 1927 model. Dad said, 'You can't drive that car until you're old enough.' You had to be sixteen to drive a car in those days. You didn't need a license, but you had to be sixteen.

"One Sunday he drove it. He took Mom for a ride in it," Festus continued. "Somewhere west of Harrodsburg a car hit him and knocked the car plumb over into a ditch. I went to Fowler's Garage later and looked in a window and there hung my Ford on Wyatt's wrecker. Boy that was some sight. And I had worked a hundred days to get it. Lucky, Dad and Mom were not hurt."

Edna was nineteen when she and Eddie were wed. During the long years of their marriage she was devoted to him. Petite at seventy-five pounds and under five feet in height, she nevertheless was hardy and resilient. Her children were born in Harrodsburg. At the time of their births, neighbors Oma Lowery and Arabelle Crum came in and "did" for Edna until the doctor arrived. After he went away, the women took over until the new mother could do for herself.

"I was never in a hospital in my life," Edna remarked to me with a smile one day, several years after Eddie's death. "People don't know nothin' now to what they used to know. Mercy! We were able to make do without all the comforts. I had a family before I had electric lights."

The reason for this visit with Edna was her eighty-eighth birthday. Still tiny, blue-eyed and white-haired, she was vibrant and attractive in a peach and lemon check, below-the-knee morning coat, and somewhat burlesque in low cut white sneakers. "I got eighty-six birthday cards," she bubbled, her eyes clear and bright. "Two more and I'd've had the same as my age."

Asked to enumerate the members of her entire family, Edna raised small, fragile palms in my direction. "Don't ask me that," she laughed. "I don't know. I've got children. I've got grandchildren. I've got great grandchildren. I've got great-great grandchildren. I've got a step-grandchild, and I've got a foster grandchild." She shook her head and dropped her hands to her lap.

At this time her home was on a hill overlooking the newly constructed four-lane highway between Bloomington and Bedford and, in the distance, the community that had been her home and Eddie's home for so many years. She enjoyed sitting before a large picture window to drink in that view. She had no dreams, no plans, no illusions about a late knight in dimming armor. She was happy in her solitude, happy with her memories, happy being who she was, and happy to be where she was.

Eddie Crum, as his son Festus had observed, was also content to live his own life, to be his own man. Yet, by his very nature, he was everyman's man, his natural talent and irrepressible drollery brightening their days with generous amounts of song and laughter. Aglow with the light of happy recollection, Festus related how his father had once again brought humor to the people of Harrodsburg.

"The Ingram boys had a big hog farm about two miles south of Harrodsburg, and they gave Dad a pig," he said. "Well, Dad put a collar on that pig, and a leash, like you would on a dog, named it 'Arnold,' and led it around town. He'd walk it over to Fowler's Garage – that was the main highway before the new four-lane was built – and he'd buy a bottle of soda pop and feed it to that pig. Just tip up the bottle in its mouth, and the pig would drink it. He gave people a lot of laughs with that pig. He kept it until it died."

When torrential rains once overflowed the ditch where Eddie had played out his dead fish caper, the Crum home, which was nearby, was inundated. He later was interviewed by a newspaper reporter about the incident. Asked to recount how he and his wife had escaped the flood waters rushing into their home, Eddie replied, "We just got in the bathtub, and while we floated around we sang, 'Over The Waves.' "

An overstuffed chair that was in the yard at the time of the flood was washed away by the racing tide. Festus explained why such a piece of furniture was outside. "Mom picked up a cushion that was on that chair and there lay a coiled snake under it," he laughed. "They just carried the chair and snake out to the yard and it was there when the flood came."

Eddie was a drinker. A sporadic one, but a drinker nevertheless. Except for Edna, who, on moral and religious grounds disapproved of alcohol, he hurt no one but himself by his imbibing. He was cursed with a stomach ulcer, and while he may have been happy in the bottle, he suffered painfully when he crawled out of it. Loving him as she did, Edna preferred that he abstain. He either wouldn't or couldn't. When the desire gripped him, he drank. After a spree, he invariably would bring a bottle home with him that he would hide in an outbuilding, or someplace else on the property. Wise to his ways, Edna would set about looking for it until she found it. She would pour its contents on the ground, leaving Eddie without the proverbial sobering hair of the dog that had bitten him.

Instead of trying to outwit the cunning Edna when he came home tipsy after one such outing, Eddie sneaked the bottle past her and into the house. Out of sight of his wife, he made himself comfortable in an easy chair. While she was busy searching the outbuildings and the rest of the Crum property for the whiskey she was certain he had brought home with him, Eddie reclined in the comfort of his own home, leisurely taking periodic pulls at the bottle under his coat. He was a rascal, to be sure, but a precious one.

Eddie was eighty-five one May and he died the following November. The year was 1971. In its November 19 issue of that year, *The Herald Telephone* newspaper carried the following five short paragraphs in its area obituaries:

Eddie Crum Sr., 85, of Harrodsburg, died Thursday afternoon at Bloomington Hospital.

He was a retired painter and musician, and a member of the Harrodsburg Church of Christ.

Survivors are the wife, Edna; two daughters Mrs. Otis (Forrest) Wright and Mrs. Phyllis W. McPike, both of Harrodsburg; three sons, Clayton, Festus and Edward Jr., all of Bloomington; fourteen grandchildren; twenty-one great grandchildren; and two great-great grandchildren.

Services will be Sunday at 2 p.m. at the Greene and Harrell Chapel, with Brother Floyd Bounds officiating. Burial will be in Clover Hill Cemetery (Harrodsburg).

Friends may call at the funeral home from 7-9 p.m. today and from 2-9 p.m. Saturday.

Ironically, the lead obituary in the paper that day was that of another painter, a Brown County artist. He was not a native Hoosier and his reputation locally was limited. Eddie Crum, by comparison, was known to scores of people in the newspaper's circulation area. Yet the lead obituary appeared under a two column headline and was accompanied by a one-column photograph.

As Festus said of his father, Eddie wouldn't have begrudged anyone anything, not even an unknown painter a bigger obituary than his own. And anyone who knew Eddie was aware that he was an artist in his own right, and that was sufficient for local memory.

Eddie, who pretended to nothing more than what he was himself, was born within two miles of Harrodsburg. He grew up in the small community, lived there, died there, and his earthly remains are buried there. His son, Eddie Jr., related a story about Eddie that seems to prove that Harrodsburg is where Eddie always wanted to be.

"He was talking with several people at Fowler's Garage one day when a northbound Greyhound bus stopped there," Eddie Jr. remembered. "The bus always stopped there to pick up or discharge passengers going north or south. Dad had been drinking and was so caught up in the talk that when the others got on the bus he just moved right on with them. He kept right on talking until the bus got near Bloomington. Then he leaned over to the driver and he said, 'Drop me off at Harrodsburg.' "

CLOSE TO HEAVEN

A contemporary maxim nurtured by some Crawford Countians suggests that anyone who cannot get to Heaven ought to at least go to English, the county seat.

So I went to English one bright, sunny day in August, 1989. In response to my knock on a strange door there I was welcomed inside and greeted with warm words and soft hugs (in that order) by two beaming, smiling ladies.

Nothing like that had ever happened to me, not even at home, and I wondered if I were not in Heaven, or pretty close to it. Had my welcomers been a few decades younger, I might have believed they were cherubim.

"Which one are you?" they chorused through the laughing salutations and cordialities of our meeting. Before I could respond, one of them added, "You don't look like any of the rest of us."

For some reason they had assumed that I was a long-lost relative. Since I wasn't, they were entitled to a responsible explanation. I offered the only one I had brought with me.

"No," I began, "I am not a relative." I looked directly at one of them, whom I learned was Ilene Jones, and said, "Your son, Red Jones, in Bloomington, told me about you. Said if I ever got to English I ought to look you up."

And to her companion I blurted, "I thought you were Red's mother, he looks so much like you."

More laughter. "I'm his aunt, Norma McKinney," she explained when she was able. "Ilene's sister. I live just over there." She leaned to one side and pointed past me in the direction of the open door.

We were still standing in the middle of Ilene Jones's living room. "Sit down," she invited. "Sit down."

From the comfort of an overstuffed chair, I further explained my visit, that I had a car serviced at Red's Auto Repair. It was there, too, I informed the two ladies, now seated opposite me, that Red had one day told me about his mother, and that it was from him that I first heard the saying, "If you can't get to Heaven you ought to at least go to English." There was more laughter.

In their eighties, the two sisters, both widows, were together much of the time. They slept at Norma's house at nighttime and, except for visits with their families, they passed the days together at Ilene's house or at Norma's.

"We cling pretty close," Norma said. She smiled at Ilene and added, "I don't know what we'd do without each other. I guess we'll stay with each other until the Lord takes me home."

"That's the only thing that'll separate us," Ilene affirmed.

The two had clung pretty close the night of a tornado warning, the memory of which was still fresh and which they related to me through tears of hilarity. As they remembered the incident, they'd heard on television that a funnel cloud had been sighted ninety miles away. But Ilene and Norma were taking no chances because it was already storming and hailing in English, and conditions for a tornado there seemed over-ripe.

"They tell you to take cover if a tornado is coming," said Ilene.

"Yes," Norma agreed. "They do. So we got under the kitchen table."

That was the start of a problem. When either of the two sisters got down, she needed help to get back up. Norma, it seems, got her help a lot sooner than she expected, and long before the all clear had been sounded.

"I was all hunkered down under the table when I took a cramp in my leg," she explained. "Tornado or no tornado, I had to get up.

"We laughed and laughed over that," she said. "Then I saw Ilene crawling out from under the table toward a chair to help support herself so she could get up. And we laughed and laughed some more."

The continuing memory added to their shared mirth, and I, having more than once suffered a cramp at the darndest times, and in the darndest places myself, was having the best laugh I'd had in weeks just from being within view of them and earshot of their infectious laughter.

As the story goes, the preacher visited a few days later and Ilene gave him a play-by-play account of that amusing episode.

"As she began telling it I got tickled again," Norma, in the grip of laughter again, spoke through tears of glee that ran down her cheeks, "and we laughed and laughed again."

Because we were all in the mood, the three of us laughed some more. So few people enjoy healthy laughter nowadays that my visit with Ilene and

Norma seemed an unusual event. For me. But apparently not for them.

"We always have a good time," Norma assured me. "We enjoy being together. When we're away from each other for a few days, we're so glad to see each other when we get back."

On the return drive from English to my office in Bloomington, I was aware of a sense of lightheartedness. Deep inside myself I felt cheered and gladdened. Could it be really true, I asked the bespectacled image that glanced back at me from the rear vision mirror, that there is something more than words to that old saying, "If you can't get to Heaven, you ought to at least go to English?"

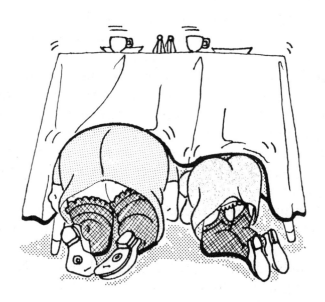

DEADLY DUEL

When the "milk of the wild cow" was still dripping freely from hidden copper boilers in the hills and woodlands of Lawrence County, two men murdered each other in a gun duel, the details of which are still steeped in mystery.

It was speculated at the time by O.D. Emerson, who then was county coroner, and Tom Brinkworth, the county prosecutor, that Ben Pierce, thirty-eight, and Brooks Collins, twenty-eight, had shot each other to death in an argument over moonshine. But the actual cause of the December 21, 1927, shooting was never learned.

There was a possibility that Ben's wife, Margaret, knew the reason or reasons behind the deadly duel. She confused the initial official investigation by hiding Ben's pistol in a bureau drawer. However, she admitted nothing.

Ben and Margaret Pierce lived in a tent in the rolling hills near Fayetteville, several miles west of Bedford. Brooks Collins lived a short distance away on a twenty-eight acre farm with his wife and two children.

Public records of the shooting revealed that on that particular Wednesday before Christmas, Ben and

37

Margaret returned to their tent from a trip to Bedford sometime during the afternoon. According to Margaret's testimony, which she gave at a hearing on the matter, Ben took up a bucket and said he was going to a spring across the road for water. Several minutes later she heard shots, she testified, and when she investigated, she found the two men dead.

When Emerson and Sheriff Harry Gordon arrived on the scene, they found the men lying about forty-five feet apart. Ben Pierce had a bullet hole over his left eye, Brooks Collins was shot through the heart. The only weapon found was a .32 caliber Colt automatic, the property of Brooks Collins. This led authorities to presume that murder and suicide had been committed. But on the following day, Gordon and Brinkworth rechecked the scene and Ben's tent. They found a .32 caliber Iver-Johnson revolver in a bureau drawer.

Margaret subsequently testified that she had removed the revolver from the death scene. It was on the ground, she told interrogators, between the legs of her dead husband, where he had fallen. This admission unravelled Emerson's autopsy enigma brought on by the discovery after the shooting of a single weapon at the scene, that had been fired once, and the presence of a .32 caliber bullet found in each of the bodies.

Newspapers and wire services around the state played the double murder as a moonshine killing and a still owner's dishonesty. Emerson, Brinkworth and Gordon made no attempt to discourage the reporting. When "rows of little brown jugs" were later found behind Brooks Collins' house, and it was learned that the two men had "run off a batch" of moonshine a week earlier, and had argued over its distribution, the three officials joined the papers in calling the shots as they appeared.

The record shows Ben Pierce and Brooks Collins argued over that batch of moonshine or the money it brought, and they ended their differences permanently. But there was more. Brinkworth learned that Margaret and Ben had had a tiff some weeks before the deadly duel, and that they had separated for a period of time. Whether it was the product of his imagination, or if he had heard whispers to lead him to believe such a thing, no one will ever know, but Ben Pierce, Brinkworth learned, believed Margaret had been consoled by Brooks Collins during that separation. This led authorities to suspect a triangle had become a possible contributing cause to the fatal shootings.

There was still more. The record notes that on the Saturday night after the Tuesday that Ben and his partner had run off the batch of moonshine, there was great merrymaking at the Collins home. A number of men from the Fayetteville area were there, and, after much drinking, a fight ensued. Collins, for some unknown reason, reportedly got into a fight with a "boy" who was there. He was beating him severely when Ben Pierce intervened and pulled him off the youth. Witnesses reported Collins telling Pierce, "No one will ever do that (interfere) again."

Were one to examine the activities of the still partners on the day before they allegedly killed each other, none of the reported facts in the case makes much sense. To wit: on December 20, 1927, Ben Pierce and Brooks Collins cut and gathered Christmas trees which they planned to sell, and split the profits.

The killings were long the major topic of discussion in Lawrence County. In the telling and retelling, the story of the Pierce-Collins duel lost some of its reported facts, and it gathered some strange distortions. Still, the backbone of the story was kept intact, and the recounting of it continues in hand-me-down style. Most of its narrators, however, omit a strange fact.

When Ben Pierce left his wife in their tent to fetch a bucket of water from the spring across the road that fateful day, he did, in fact, go to the spring. And he did fill the bucket with water, for it was found at the spring the next day, its contents frozen solid.

Was it after he had filled the bucket that Ben Pierce himself decided to seek out Brooks Collins? Was he surprised in the midst of that innocent chore? Was he called away from it? Was he carrying a revolver? The investigation answered none of these questions.

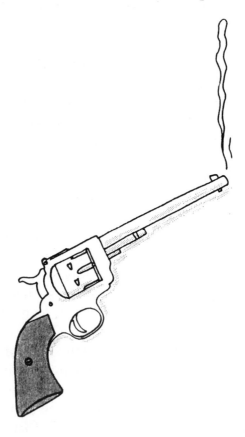

PEGGY HOLLER

When Clem Toliver was alive he used to say the road that climbed and twisted for a mile and a half through Martin County wilderness between the Jones place and the Freeman house, was the longest "street" he ever saw. Clem ought to have known. He'd walked the distance many times on his visits to the post office, which, depending on the whim of voters, was either at one end of that road or the other.

"When the Democrats were in," Ruby Toliver, Clem's widow recalled one day, "the post office was in my father's store which was at one end of that road. His name was Richard M. Jones. When the Republicans were in control, Charlie Freeman had the post office at his house, which was at the other end. And it moved that way from one end of that road to the other."

Mrs. Toliver and I were seated at the table in the kitchen of her "Windswept Farm" home near the community of Rusk, in Martin County. "This place is really windswept," she said of the name she had given the farm more than a quarter century earlier. "When everybody else is burning up with the heat, this place is the coolers. The wind really sweeps through here," she pointed beyond the picture window to the swaying trees outside.

41

The thought of being cool added to the comfort of the indoors, for it was a very cold, windy February day on the other side of the kitchen window. I had come to interview Mrs. Toliver about a family history she was compiling. In it she had given her father the distinction of having been the first postmaster at Rusk. He was a "hot" Democrat, she said of him, Freeman was an equally hot Republican, but they remained good friends and neighbors, and attended the same church.

"Dad settled in Rusk with my mother, Mary Waggoner, and opened a store there after their marriage in 1891. The post office was established and he was made postmaster a year later," she began a brief synopsis of her work.

Rusk, which is in Lost River Town/ship, was the home of Audrian and Chloe Phillips, cousins to Mrs. Toliver. Though Audrian was often referred to as "The Mayor of Rusk," the real star of the settlement was Mrs. Toliver's father, she said.

"He had the store," she added, leaving the impression that, by virtue of this position, he was given special standing in the community. "The mail came there three days a week. At the back of the store he had a little drug store where you could buy quinine, castor oil, and asafetida, and where he kept whiskey for snakebite and snorts. He was a blacksmith, he operated a grist mill and telephone exchange, and he was also the dentist."

Richard M. Jones was more. In 1910 he was admitted to the Indiana Bar, and he practiced law at Rusk and in French Lick. "He believed in pushing ahead," his daughter said of him. To illustrate this and the extent of his education, she said, "He had all the McGuffy readers when he was in school, from the first through the sixth one."

Recalling her father's early practice of dentistry, Mrs. Toliver recounted that forceps used for extracting teeth were called "pullicans." When as a little girl she would see them resting in their glass enclosed case in her father's general store, she would shudder in fear.

"Dad would take dental patients out into the yard, along with a kitchen chair, where they could spit," she frowned as she spoke. "He didn't give them anything, not even a snort. He'd just pull their teeth. Oh, I'll tell you, when I'd see those pullicans in that case I'd just shake from fright. And when I watched him pull the neighbors' teeth I was always so happy it wasn't me."

Mrs. Toliver was born in Rusk in 1901, one of six Jones children. In those early days there were three modes of travel into and out of the settlement: afoot, horseback, or by wagon. "My first car ride was in 1914," she remembered. "Dad bought a Model-T Ford on the Third of July, and after supper that night, we went for a ride. I was so happy. I can still see myself sitting in that car, all smiles."

The next morning, Mary Jones fixed a picnic lunch and the family drove off in the new Model-T to the much advertised Fourth of July Celebration at French Lick. "That car would die on the hills and Dad would have to get out and crank it," Mrs. Toliver laughed. "And backwards we would go, down the hill."

In spite of their father's several talents, the Jones kids of Rusk grew up poor, she said. "And so did everybody else. But we'd sit around the dining room table at night and my father would read a chapter or two from the Bible, and then we'd sing together. We really didn't mind being poor. Our main dish at meals was a pot of soup. Sometimes we had cornbread with milk over it. We had a relative who loved cornbread smothered in onions and soaked in grease fryings, right out of the skillet. We went to Quinn School, a one-room school with eight grades. I taught there after I became a teacher, and at another one-roomer named Hawkins School, and then at a school in French Lick Township. When we went to Quinn we took our lunches in a six-quart bucket – the six of us – but we wouldn't eat with each other at school. I remember one time we had ham, sorghum, cookies and blackberries. We had to climb a rail fence on the way to school and I spilled my lunch. My bread and cookies were soaked with blackberry juice," she laughed.

Mrs. Toliver then told me about the witch's ball. Uncle John G. Jones and his wife, Sarah, lived in a remote place called Peggy Holler. They kept sheep, and when they sheared them they stored the wool in the tiny attic of their small woodland house. Later, when they made preparations to take the wool to a carder, they were surprised to find most of it gone. All that remained were several small wool balls. Examining one, Uncle John pulled it apart and found a cocklebur at its core. He tore another apart, and another, and each wool ball was wound tightly around a cocklebur.

Uncle John and Sarah lived in a period when many people were superstitious and were easily frightened by the slightest mystery. Sarah was one of them. She confided her fear to Uncle John. "My mother," she intoned to her husband, "never said that she believed in ghosts or such things. But my mother said she had seen strange things in her time, and my mother was never known to tell a lie. And this is strange."

Whatever Sarah might have said in addition to that, if she said anything at all, has been lost in the retelling of this story. It is known that the woman's foreboding led to the destruction of all except one of the wool balls. They were thrown into a fire Uncle

John had built in the yard. The single survivor was placed in a clay pitcher and covered with a lid. Sarah related the story of shearing sheep as often as the opportunity presented itself. Each time she told it, she would make some reference to witches. And each time she told the tale, she would end it with a moving account of the burning of all but one of the wool balls. She would then lower her voice and in hushed tones tell her listeners that the single wool ball was safe in a covered pitcher in her home in Peggy Holler.

Though she never said so, it was assumed that Sarah believed a witch in the guise of a wool-covered cocklebur was imprisoned in that clay pitcher. One day when Uncle John returned to Peggy Holler from a trip to Shoals, he lifted the lid of the pitcher and saw that it was empty, the wool ball was gone. He called to his wife. "Sarah," he shouted, "where is the witch's ball?" When Uncle John showed her the empty pitcher Sarah nearly fainted. Later, as he set out to do his evening chores, Uncle John shouted to his wife from outside the house. "Sarah, here it is, right here on the ground. How did it get out here?"

Neither she nor her husband could answer that question. How that ball got out into the yard is still a mystery. Frightened, Sarah watched from a distance while Uncle John returned the wool ball to the pitcher and replaced the lid. She had all but predicted something like this might happen. She was certain now that the wool ball was a witch. In the days that followed, the story goes, Uncle John would find the wool ball in the yard, in the barnlot, the barn, the garden – everywhere. Sarah would always watch from a safe distance while he would return it to the clay pitcher and replace the lid. The continued mysterious escapes of the wool ball became too much for Sarah to bear. She presumed upon Uncle John to build another fire in the yard and throw it into the flames. "It was the only way, you know," Sarah would often say later, "that a witch can be destroyed."

Peggy Holler, a lengthy north-south depression in the earth flanking Lost River, supposedly got its name from an incident that occurred there many years ago. A matron whose name was Peggy, reportedly was murdered there. The story has more than one version, but this is the one told me by Mrs. Toliver while we sat in her kitchen.

Peggy and her husband lived in the small two-room house with a lean-to kitchen which later became Uncle John and Sarah's home. There were no witnesses, but it was presumed that a back-peddler climbed the rise to the little house one day and knocked on the door. It was speculated that Peggy was so charmed by the pots and pans and the spices and yard goods and tablecloths the man carried that she incautiously opened her door to him. When her husband returned home that evening, he found Peggy lying on a blood-spattered floor, her head severed from her body and nowhere to be found.

Crazed by the sight and his subsequent fruitless search of the house for his wife's head, Peggy's husband fled into the night calling repeatedly, "Peg-eee! Peg-eee!" There were few homes in Peggy Holler at that time but eventually the searching husband arrived at one, and by dawn the entire countryside had learned of the woman's violent death. Peggy's husband refused to accept the headless corpse as the body of his wife. And until his death some years later, he could be heard nightly as he trekked the long hollow calling, "Peg-eee! Peg-eee!" Those who heard the plaintive calls would sadly observe to one another, "Listen, he's still hollerin' for Peggy." It was just a matter of time until the place became known as Peggy Holler.

Strange things began happening in Peggy Holler after that. For instance, tall and gangly Bruce Reeves was walking home one midnight when a limb suddenly snapped and fell off a tree. He ran the whole length of Peggy Holler, getting out of there as fast as he could. A Union soldier from French Lick looking for Civil War deserters was shot to death there. The Archer Gang allegedly traveled there, and many tales have been told about those passages. Because of their superstitions, people were frightened of Peggy Holler and it took little to get a tale started about the woodsy place. Hazel Bullard, who enjoyed playing tricks on people and making them laugh, used to take a shortcut through there to visit Inez Shipman. One day, just for the fun of it, she dressed in strange looking clothes before setting out to visit her friend who lived on the other side of Peggy Holler. On the way she saw a gang of timbermen at work. Recognizing some of them, she approached at a slow walk. As she neared one of them, he raised an axe and threatened, "You git!" She knew the man but it was obvious he did not see through her disguise. Before she could say anything the man again threatened her with the axe. "You git, or I'll kill you!" he shouted. Still at a safe distance, Hazel stopped and in as spooky a voice as she could muster she droned, "You can't kill Peggy Holler!" The frightened timbermen dropped their axes and saws and fled.

As girls, Mrs. Toliver and Inez rode bareback on big draft horses through the hollow. Mrs. Toliver couldn't remember having seen any witches, but she did remember that it was a scary experience. She insisted that I see the place for myself and we climbed into my pickup truck. We drove into Peggy Holler from the north, and at its south end she showed me where she used to live, on Powell Valley Road, on the banks of Buck Creek. We stopped at what was left of the old Hawkins School, and Mrs. Toliver said she had taught there in 1924. I took a photo of her standing in front of the old hulk.

With Mrs. Toliver's knowledge of the trail, we were able to get past all the witches and the haunts and scary things in Peggy Holler without incident. But when she directed me to drive high above Lost River, on a tree-lined ancient roadway covered with ice, I was just about as spooked as anyone had ever got there.

THE PROPHET

Folklore had it that if a stranger wanted to find the Old Dutch Church, which is situated in rural Monroe County between Ellettsville and Stinesville, he should, to facilitate that undertaking, ask directions of "any teenager with a girlfriend." The implication being, of course, that the remote churchyard was a favorite sparking place of young lovers. On a January morning in 1978, a morning suffused with bright, frozen sunlight, I was unable to find such a guide. So, I settled for what I decided was a half loaf; I stopped at Stinesville to ask directions in the Bob Summitt Grocery Store.

"It's right over here, on Red Hill Road," Bob said, gesturing, it seemed to me, toward both the rear wall and the ceiling of the store simultaneously.

"Just go right out here," chipped in store lounger Don Taylor, former fire chief in Stinesville and fabricator of circular iron stairways. "Right out there, that way," he said, carelessly flinging out a hand and pointing, I thought, toward the ceiling.

"You'll come to a railroad crossing," he continued. "You'll go along until you turn over another one, and then you'll go across this concrete swag – you'll have to ford the creek – and then you'll be there."

I studied both Bob and Don for a time, wondering the while if I shouldn't wait for some teenager with a girlfriend to come along. In my rovings around rural Indiana, I had received better directions to remote places from horses and cows that were safely separated from me by barbed wire fences.

It was not my first time in the store. While I stood there trying to make up my mind about Bob and Don, I noticed that the heart of Stinesville – the store – had been remodeled. The place seemed smaller, with a dropped ceiling, and a larger post office. The smaller area and the dropped ceiling, I was told, served to cut by half the cost of heating the store. The enlarged post office, however, contained the same one hundred and five boxes the previous, smaller room did. There were one hundred and three families in town, two more than in 1963. Because there was no home delivery, ninety-six of them, give or take a few, rented boxes in the post office.

Seeking to be of further help, Bob volunteered that, "If Maudeline Duckworth has finished with it – she has all my stuff on that old church. You could read it . . ."

Before he could finish telling me much more about Maudeline Duckworth and his written information about the old church, there was a racket at the door and a man walked in. He was shouting that Indiana would beat Iowa by ten points in that night's basketball game. In the same breath, he added that Indiana would take Illinois by eight points in the following Saturday's game, and that – by golly – Indiana wouldn't lose to any Big Ten team "this season, and does anybody want to bet that I'm wrong."

It was quite startling, him bursting in and shouting like that, and also quite a mouthful. Bob looked at me, he looked around at the gathering of loungers, then back at me, and he said, "Meet Cedrick Walden.

When Cedrick says they'll do it, they usually do it."
The man called Cedrick agreed, and added, "But
sometimes I have to bet awful hard for them to do it."

I then learned that Cedrick (pronounced ked-rick)
bet Bob so hard on the Indiana-Illinois game two
years earlier that the Hoosiers won by twenty-eight
points, eight more than Cedrick had predicted. Bob
was so impressed that within two minutes after the
game had ended he took his losings over to Cedrick's
house, opened the door, threw the money inside, and
drove away.

"I was sitting there on the bed," Cedrick recalled
his surprise. "I hadn't even got the television turned
off yet, it was that soon after the game. I could see
him driving up. Then he come up and he just opened
the door and throwed that money in. And I heard him
holler, 'Here it is!' "

Bob's unexpected action was about as surprising to
Cedrick as was the backside blaze of Ralph Parrish's
coveralls to him when he got too near the stove. Ralph
had come to the store earlier. So had six year old Mikey
Taylor. The little boy put a nickel on the counter and
asked Bob, "What can I get for this?" Bob, ignoring an
opportunity to enlighten the youngster on the effects of
inflation, suggested the youngster tilt up his forehead
and he would give him a kiss on it.

In just a few minutes, I learned more about
Cedrick. An avid Hoosier fan, he attended games at
Assembly Hall only when he could obtain anything
better than a seat in the bleachers. He was sixty-five
years old and had retired from working in limestone
quarries. He'd grown up in and around Stinesville
and, as a boy in junior high school, played basketball
for teacher-coach Orla McPhetteridge. As a young
man, he helped to haul the stone for the old Stinesville school's gym in 1926. The entire structure,

school and gym, was destroyed by fire in 1934. Kids attended classes in the town's homes and stores until the loss could be replaced.

Basketball was once played on the first floor of the Odd Fellows Hall, the space occupied by Bob's store, exactly where we were talking and lounging near the counter. The "Liar's Bench," Cedrick informed us, was the bleacher section. Since we were gathered on hallowed planking, the talk, which was periodically interrupted by the desultory announcements of new arrivals, naturally kept returning to basketball. Big Ten stuff.

Cedrick was in the mood to make a comparison. "The rest of the Big Ten teams are just ordinary," he said. "And Indiana is so tough no ordinary team is going to take them."

When he was told that this column would not reach print until *after* the Iowa game, and I therefore could not make public his prediction before then, Cedrick said I shouldn't worry. Indiana would get right in there and play, anyway, and do as they're told, and win, and that their coach could take any team in the Big Ten and make them "as good as Indiana is right now." Jerking his chin down in an affirmative motion, he added, "He's that smart of a basketball man. He eats basketball. He sleeps basketball. He dreams basketball. He's got a basketball head on him. And that makes him the best coach in the whole United States."

Last season Cedrick called every game but three, and he lost each of those by only one point. After that everybody backed away from challenging his opinion, his faith in Indiana, and his money.

The front door kept opening and closing and among those who joined the gathering were Winifred Prather and Norman Walls, as well as Gary Summitt,

Basil Walden, and Danny Bowman. Little Mikey Taylor, who at last had decided to refuse a kiss on his forehead, had successfully traded his nickel for a grape flavored lollipop. By this time, I was biting into a store-made sandwich of Old Fashion Loaf with cheese and pickles, and swiggin a soda, and was in the process of concluding Cedrick was some kind of local prophet to be reckoned with. As someone had said, he was not only good at picking winning basketball teams and coaches, he was also hard to beat at shooting craps. I was cautioned against having any truck with him.

Maudeline Duckworth was not at home, or she at least did not answer the telephone when Bob dialed her number. After more pointless directions from the gang in the store, I left there and was lucky enough to find Red Hill Road. From there, two men, an old one and a young one, who were cutting brush along the roadside, directed me to the Old Dutch Church Road. I crossed the railroad tracks and found Don Taylor's "swag" across muddy Jack's Defeat Creek. Eventually, I came to Old Dutch Community Church, and what was left of a frame building that was the *old* church, and the cemetery beyond.

I had learned from an aging newspaper clipping that the older building was constructed of logs in 1845, and was known as St. John's Lutheran Church. The windowless remains showed evidence of having been covered at one time with clapboard siding, then yellowing with age. In better times the building was used by various denominations, "So long," I quote from the aging newspaper clipping, "as God dwelt there." From what I saw of the place, He apparently abandoned it for the newer concrete block church after it was built. Probably because it was warmer in there than in the windowless older building.

NO CHANGES

Few people are fortunate enough to stay alive for as many years as Delbert and Hazel Mathews were married. It was December 4, 1913, when Uncle Newt Dixon tied the two together at his Tunnelton home. They'd traveled from Budah, a few miles west. As Hazel Greene, she'd grown up in that neighborhood, the youngest of a family of four brothers and two sisters. Delbert also was reared near that small community, in the area of Dixon Chapel. Uncle Newt, in addition to being a justice of the peace, taught music, and Hazel was one of his pupils.

At age eighty-five, and after sixty-eight years of marriage, she was the pianist for the sing-alongs held at Hospitality House, in Bedford, where she and her husband lived. "I play the organ, too, and I used to play the piano and organ for the services at the White River Baptist Church," she said. "And I used to also call square dances. I got to be pretty good at it, too, I liked it that well."

She came by calling naturally. Her father, John Greene, was probably one of the best square dance callers to ever raise his voice in eastern Lawrence County, on either side of White River. As a girl, Hazel danced to his calling, as she also did in later life. "I loved to square dance," she said looking fondly back over the years. "I loved it so much, and I got to be such a fool about it, I'd square dance every time I got the chance."

Delbert was there with her, enjoying the fun too. But he shook his head at the memory stirred to life by his wife's words, and claimed awkwardness. "That was my problem," he said. "And I was never too much of a dancer because of it." When children visited the residents of Hospitality House, Hazel often played the piano for them. If Delbert felt up to it, he played along on the harmonica. "But," he shrugged, "it takes a little more wind to play one of these things than I have right now to keep it agoing."

Delbert, who was eighty-nine when we talked, reared his family of six children on a forty-acre farm, with an assist from his talents as a carpenter. "That's what I did most of, carpentering," he said. "Until I got too old and stiff to be any good at it anymore." While he carpentered, Hazel and the children farmed. One of those children, Chester Mathews, recalled the family's early years.

"We raised our living on that place," he said. "It was a lot of fun, and a lot of hard work. I remember one time that Dad put out four acres of beans – white beans. When they were ready, we harvested them by the bush and put the whole thing down in a sack. When the sack was filled, we beat on it with a stick, or anything else we could find. We actually beat the beans out of the bushes. Then we dumped them out on a bedsheet and separated the beans from the chaff and dust." Chester also recalled plowing four acres for corn with a six-inch breaking plow pulled by a single horse. "We were a big family," he said. "We had to work hard, every one of us. But we all had a good time."

Delbert and Hazel agreed it was a good time, raising a big family. "There were some ups and downs," Delbert said. Sickness, hard times, lean times. And there was World War II that took the four Mathews boys away from home. One served with the Marines, one was in the Army, and two served in the Navy. After the war, they returned safely. Son Leon lived at Budah on the family farm, Vernon had retired and lived in Florida, Clyde was in Marion, and Chester lived at Guthrie. Each of the brothers had a wife named Mary. Their sisters, Ilene Mathews Jenkins, and Helen Mathews Holt, resided in Bedford and Avoca, respectively.

What is it like to spend sixty-eight years – a virtual lifetime – in marriage, with one man or one woman? "What a question?" retorted Hazel. After a moment's thought, she added, "I'm proud of it."

Delbert had his own answer. "I just never paid much attention to it. Time just goes on, and I take it as it comes," he said.

One thing, sixty-eight years is enough time to reach some conclusions. With the benefit of hindsight would the Mathews, if they could, have changed any part of their lives together?

"If I could?" Hazel asked, totally aware of the futility of such a thought. "I suppose a few little things," she said finally. "I'd marry Delbert again. He's been a good husband. And we've had a fine time in our lives."

Delbert pondered the question for some time, then drawled, "Well, I don't know what I would change. I worked hard all my life. And I spent all the money I could get ahold of." He looked at Hazel and smiled. "But I don't see where I'd do anything different than I've done. There've been a lot of good things happen to us. The best has been just living together in this old world."

"BUD" PENNINGTON

Joseph D. Pennington made his way from North Carolina to Indian Creek Township in Greene County, Indiana, as a part of a wagon train. Along the way, he had many experiences. One, an incident at a trading post one night, he passed on to his grandchildren. One of them, Fred "Bud" Pennington, recounted that incident to me.

"The man who ran the trading post said to a man in the wagon train when they got there, 'I've got a present for you. Been waiting for you to come along so I could give it to you,' " Bud began.

Cautioning the trading post owner that he'd never before been that far west, the man from the wagon train insisted that a mistake was about to be made. "You can't have a present for me. And you couldn't have been waiting for me," Bud quoted from his grandfather's account, "because I've never been here before and you don't even know me."

"I know that," the story continues with the trader's response. "But a salesman came in here months ago and sold me a whole lot of things. He gave me a big bean pot and he said, 'I want you to give this to the ugliest man you see as a present from me.' And,

57

mister, you are the ugliest man I ever did see, and the bean pot is yours."

At that point in the story, Bud paused to laugh heartily. Then he continued: "Grandfather used to tell that story, and he'd say, 'Every time we cooked beans on that trail after that, someone would holler to bring out the *ugly-pot.*' "

At this time, Bud was two months from marking his seventy-fourth birthday. He was a cheery, rotund man with bright blue eyes. He wore an old, blue and white striped billed cap, time-worn Big Mac bib-over-alls and a faded khaki shirt. The latter two were patched in a half dozen places with scrap materials of various colors, all revealing Bud's own crude hand stitching to hold them in place.

He had paused again to dig his fingers into a paper and foil Peachey Chewing Tobacco pouch and stuff some shredded sweet-smelling tobacco into his mouth. He worked it around with his tongue until he had it placed exactly where he wanted it. Then he began recounting the story that had brought me to his home on Moore's Creek, where he "batched" and cared for a sickly younger brother, Desmond.

"No, it wasn't grandfather who killed that bear over there in Greene County," he began. "You see, Grand-father was a bootmaker. That was back when they put soles on with wooden pegs and used hog hairs dipped in bees wax to tie the inner sole to the boot tops.

"Well, one night this man knocked on Grand-father's door," Bud said. "He'd been on his way there to pick up a pair of boots he had Grandfather make for him. He was pretty excited, and he hollered at Grandfather, 'Do you have any torches ready?' They used torches then instead of lanterns when they went out at night, you see, and they generally had some made up ahead.

"Grandfather told him he did, but he wondered what all the excitement was about. This man told him, then. He said, 'I was making my way over here and a big bear grabbed aholt of me and very nearly hugged me to death. He wasn't mad, but he was akilling me to eat. I somehow got my hand into my pocket and got my pocketknife out and opened it with one hand. Then I just pushed it into that bear and he let go of me and fell dead.'

"Well, they got their torches lit and went back out there, and sure enough, along the trail the way that man'd come, they found the dead bear. And that's about all there is to the bear story. Except that for a good while after that they ate bear meat, for they took all the meat off'n that animal that was fit to eat," Bud said.

"After Grandmother died, there in Greene County," he continued unexpectedly on a different subject, "Grandfather learned of a young widow living over by Smithville who had several children. He rode over there and suggested to her that it would be a convenience to both of them if they was to get married. That's the way some people got married and remarried back then, you know. When she asked him how old he was, he took off about twenty years. She found out about it much later. But, at the time, Grandfather pointed out, it was so far from Greene County to Smithville for a courtship of any kind that if she was agreeable to it, they ought to get married real quick. So, she really didn't have time to study about his age much before they got married. I guess Grandfather was a young looking man to have got by with that. But we was kids then and we thought he was old."

A vogue of early Hoosiers was to wear boots that "skreeked," Bud observed. "People'd have the bootmaker fix them so that they would make a skreekin' sound. Grandfather would take and fill one goose quill with sulfur and fit another over the open end and put them between the outer and inner soles of boots or slippers. And, every time you took a step, they would skreek." He smiled while he took a moment to finger fresh Peachey into his mouth.

"I was born right over the hill and up the holler a little ways," he pointed toward the east, "on Baxter's Branch. I remember when we was kids what we'd get for Christmas – a striped stick of candy apiece. They was nine of us, but one died of brain fever. At least that's what they called it in those days. You know," he paused to spit Peachey juice on the ground at his feet, "there was a feller here from the folklore place at the univers'ty one time. He wanted to know what the most exciting thing was that ever happened to me." Bud ran the back of a hand over his chin, below a broadening grin. "I told him that knowing tomorrow I was going to town to get new shoes for winter was the most exciting thing that ever happened to me. If I knew that the night before we was to go to town, I wouldn't sleep all night, I'd be so excited. Another feller from over there came with a tape recorder and asked me if I ever saw any witches. I said the only ones I ever saw is them that rides on brooms in pictures."

Bud's age and the years he spent in rural Monroe County made him an attraction for folklore students. They called at his home each school year and pumped him for as much old Indiana as he could remember. One was a Lebanese girl, the only person ever to write and thank him for his assistance.

"She wrote and told me that it was good to be back home with her family and friends in Lebanon. But she said she still loved Americky, and that she'd always remember me and my hospitality," Bud said.

Five years before my visit with him, Bud was taken to Bloomington Hospital for emergency surgery. "I can't expect to have the best of everything," he confided his feelings to a nurse after his arrival there. "I'm an uninvited guest, and uninvited guests shouldn't expect the best someone has to offer." Then he said apologetically, "If I get hateful, it's because I don't know what I'm doing."

If his hosts were dubious about what to expect from him, they soon learned what everyone who was ever around him for any length of time already knew. Bud Pennington was a fine person who loved easily and was easy to love. By the time he had recuperated enough to leave the hospital, he had so ingratiated himself that his departure brought tears to the eyes of some of his nurses; they were that sorry to see him leave.

He had spent most of his life caring and cooking for himself and his brother, Desmond. Until he found a commercial mix that was satisfactory, he made biscuits daily from scratch. "But now," he said, "I buy a lot of Marthy White's mix and just add a little water. I grease my pan, of course, and they just fall apart, they're so good."

He still could read the newspaper without the aid of glasses. "And," he spoke of more good fortune, "I can hear as well now as when I was five. See here." He pulled the package of Peachey from a pocket in the patched overalls and extended it toward me. "I can read the fine print on this, and the sun ain't even very bright right now either."

We were standing in Bud's yard. Some weathered gray sheds, four or five of the stand-up, walk-in kind, were stacked from back to front with firewood. There were stacks of firewood around the yard. Across the road from us a pile of seasoned firewood rose from the green of a field next to Bud's large garden patch. "I'll bet I've got enough firewood to last five years," he said. Pointing to the many trees that grew on his place, he said, "When I don't have anything else to do, I cut wood, and I've got six power saws that I cut it with."

He led the way around a neatly stacked rick of wood to the corner of one of the outbuildings and pointed to one of his power saws, a bow saw hanging from a tree. "Got three of them and three crosscut saws," he said, again squirting Peachey juice on the ground. "And it takes a lot of *power* to operate them," he laughed as he went into a Charles Atlas stance. "Believe me," he said.

Bud had no car, no truck; he did not drive and depended on his two legs to carry him miles to a grocery store. A friend sometimes took him there in his car. There was a time when he didn't have to worry about going to the store. What people didn't grow in their gardens, a huckster brought in his wagon, and later in his truck, to their doors, he said.

"I remember that they used to carry three kinds of chewing gum. One would break up in little pieces in your mouth, and you had to chew it real fast to make it stick together in a wad. But there was another that was called 'Kiss Me If You Will,' and the huckster always had fun out of that when the women would ask for it. Then there was another that was called 'Long Tom' and it was nothing but paraffin," he said.

Until the old man's death a few years earlier, Bud doctored with George Mitchell. A physician who lived into his nineties, Mitchell had a small office in his home at Smithville. From there he enjoyed a wide practice in rural Lawrence and Monroe counties. Bud remembered an ancient dentist's chair that was in the doctor's office. "He told me one day many years ago, 'I got that chair from old Doc Simmons, and it's going to run me through.' And it did. He had it there until he died," Bud said.

He then related a story told him by Dr. Mitchell. "He told me there was these two families living across the road from each other, and the one family was always acalling him to doctor their kids. The other family, he told me, never called him. He said those children were always out, like pigs in the cold, rain, snow and sunshine. When it was cold, they'd have lambs legs hangin' from their noses to their mouths, and when it was hot, they'd be covered with flies. He said the woman across the road from those kids asked him one day, 'How come I try to take care of my children and they're always sick. And those kids across the road run like animals and they're never sick?' And old Doc, he said, 'Lady, that's the trouble with your children, they're getting too much pertection.' "

Bud hurried to add to that story that he was not giving advice to mothers of young children. Advice, he observed, doesn't necessarily have to be good, or bad. To illustrate his point, he told this little story. "Two fellers, bums, sitting by the road one day atalkin'. One says to the other, 'I guess I should've taken all the advice people tried to give me. Maybe I wouldn't be sitting here by the road right now.' The other fellow looked at him and said, 'I don't know. I took everybody's advice, and I'm here, too.' "

Before the coming of Lake Monroe, Bud farmed more than a hundred acres in Perry Township and another hundred acres adjoining Salt Creek Township. Most of the land is now under water. "I can remember when we used to have to keep fires aburnin' around the fields day and night to keep the wild turkeys from eating our crops," he said. "There was even a turkey trap up the ridge near Baxter's place. They called that place Turkey Pen Point."

Like the healthy children of Dr. Mitchell's story, Bud, as a farmer, was always outside in all kinds of weather. A passerby stopped one time to say, "I see you crawlin' around in your garden. I see you cuttin' wood. I see you out in the rain and in the snow. Aren't you afraid you'll get sick." Bud quelled the man's fears, and then he told him, "I don't work hard, but I work steady. If'n I'd quit, I'd not last no time."

In addition to working the live-long day around his place, and doing the cooking for himself and his brother, Bud also helped his neighbors with their butchering. His talents were widely known, and many sought his help at butchering time.

Since he had early in our visit recounted a story about his grandfather killing a bear in Greene County, Bud probably figured he should end our visit with the story about his father, Samuel Pennington, killing a wildcat in Monroe County. At any rate, he pushed right on with an account of it.

"He was riding on horseback, coming home from a grist mill in Smithville with a sack of meal slung across the horse's back behind the saddle," he began. "All of a sudden, from out of a tree, this wildcat jumped on him. It was winter, and they had awful well-built clothes back then, but the cat's claws cut right through those clothes and tore my father's shoulder.

"Well, the horse bolted," he continued, "and my father hung on all right, but the sack of meal fell off. And that cat filled up on it. My father got home and got some men together and they went back and killed that cat. He was so filled up with meal, he was too lazy to put up much of a fight." Bud emphasized the animal's lethargy by leaning to one side and directing another stream of brown Peachey juice to the ground.

As I prepared to leave him, Bud asked if I'd like some radishes, and I said I would. We walked across the road to his big garden. There I saw purplish-white bulbs about the size of softballs with lush green tops jutting up from the ground. "Those sure are big radishes," I exclaimed. Bud looked at me sorrowfully and said with disdain, "Them's turnips." So that I would see, and forever know the difference, he gave me both radishes and turnips to take home with me.

TENSE NIGHT

There probably have been few nights in the quiet, sparsely populated Whitehall neighborhood as tense and expectant as the night Charlie Keilbach's black angus cow underwent a Caesarean section.

Charlie and his wife, Helen, lived on State Road 48, across from the Richland Church of Christ. Their home, a two story farmhouse with Indiana limestone columns and balusters across the front porch, and pine trees filling the yard with their dark green boughs outspread in welcome, gave the place a warmth of invitation and temptation to any curious passerby. In a sideyard barnlot a collection of farm wagons, tractors, plows and White Rock hens was clearly visible.

"I've never lived on a farm, but I get the feeling that I'm coming home every time I approach this place," I told Charlie and Helen in their living room after satisfying months of curiosity and gnawing fascination by knocking on their front door one morning. "I've always wanted to just turn into the driveway and come in."

I remember Charlie as a pleasant man; a big man with large, powerful forearms and hands, who had

66

spent a lifetime working as a hooker in limestone quarries. He still held a job as hooker, and he also worked the farm. Looking at him, it occurred to me that the out-of-doors that surrounded him on both jobs – the sun, wind, rain, the cold, but mostly the sun – was etched in the flesh of his face.

Neither he nor Helen minded me knocking on their door in the middle of the morning. Of course, Helen complained that "The house is in a mess," a reaction of most women who are surprised by company. But what may have appeared a mess to her was to me the warm lived-in appearance of a house without which a visitor is constrained by a stiff awkwardness, even fear.

But she was an enjoyable hostess, and she could attend past tragedies with touches of humor, such as a serious operation, or the time the hogs got out and she stepped in a hole while trying to corral them and ended up in a cast for a year or more. There were no hogs on the farm when I visited there.

There were about forty-five chickens, most of them White Rocks, and four roosters. Charlie and Helen had butchered about a dozen roosters a few days earlier and stored them in a freezer for future use. They did have one little red hen. Not the one that found a bag of flour and had tried to carry it home by herself; a little red hen that laid little green eggs. Counting those, the couple were collecting about twenty-six eggs a day from the flock. But the hens didn't all lay every day. Helen informed me that hens will go for long periods without laying. "They get laid out," she explained.

Like most farms, this one had its dog, an attractive mixture of shepherd and collie named "Laddie," a very intelligent animal. It was limping and Charlie asked the animal – yes, asked Laddie – to lie down so that he might examine his paw. The dog lay down and Charlie began checking the sore paw. Laddie growled softly, a deep-down sound, to let Charlie know that it hurt each time he touched the paw. It was like a doctor-patient communication, with Charlie, the doctor, softly asking questions, and Laddie, the patient, responding in the only way he knew how – the deep-down sound. Charlie and Helen also had some cats – Fluffy, Missy, Tom and Snowball.

And, of course, they had Aberdeen Angus cattle, thirty head at that time, since Charlie had recently sold thirteen. One of the thirteen was the cow and another was her calf who, together, had brought about the tense, eventful night for the Keilbachs. Helen kept saying that it all happened because the cow was bred when she was too young. Whatever the reason, it became apparent to Charlie that night that the black cow could not calve normally. He telephoned veterinarian Drew Stewart.

"When he came out," Charlie began recounting the ensuing events of that night, "we rolled her over on her back and tied her legs to the barn rafters, so she couldn't move. 'Doc' Stewart had the rope; he carried all that kind of stuff in his truck. Then he gave her a shot, and then he cut that cow open and took the calf out of her."

Helen interrupted his narration. "He wouldn't let me come to the barn and watch," she said of her husband. "We had to stay in here and play euchre while all the excitement was going on."

Charlie smiled and resumed his story. "Then he sewed her up. There's three layers of skin to sew up on a cow. It took him a right-smart. He charged me seventy dollars. But we were out there several hours. Then, when he got in his truck to leave, he called his wife on his radio and said, 'It's a boy. Mother and son are doing fine.' "

Helen nursed the new bull calf for a few days from a bucket with a monstrously large nipple sticking out from its bottom. "But, he wanted his mommy," she recalled. And, animal nature being what it is, the cow recovered fast enough for the new calf to obtain its milk from her."

"I thought I'd lost money on that calf," Charlie said with a shake of his head. A smile broke over his weathered face and he added, "But you know, when I took those thirteen cattle to market, that little dude fetched me a hundred and forty-four dollars."

JOT DIEHL

Ray Goodman once said Earl Turner's store in Needmore couldn't begin to hold all the Granger pipe tobacco
that Jot Diehl smoked in his lifetime. For many years
Jot would walk down the hill from his white frame
house above Earl's store just about every day. He'd
select one of two backless benches there, pick out a
shiny spot, and sit with his back against the wall. Then
he'd take out his pipe, fill it up, light it up, and strike
up a conversation with Earl, or with another lounger
like himself. Depending on how long they talked, Jot
would relight the pipe a dozen or more times.

"I'm seventy-one, and I knew that man all my life,
and he always smoked a pipe," Earl said from a space
he himself occupied on one of the benches one summer afternoon many years ago. "There's no telling
how much Granger he's smoked in that time."

"This store," Ray then waved a hand around the
small grocery store and gasoline filling station, "could
never begin to hold it all."

"I'll tell you something else," Earl continued. "There
wasn't a nicer guy in all this world than Jot Diehl."

"He was a fine man," Ray agreed, his chin moving
up and down in affirmation.

Before going any farther with this it ought to be made clear that I'm not writing about Jot Diehl because he did some spectacular thing in his lifetime. I'm not and he didn't. Unless, of course, you might want to imply that working in a stone quarry a whole lifetime is something spectacular. Few people would believe that. You might want to say that being a father is spectacular, which Jot was. But there are those who will hurry to say fathers are all over the place, so what's spectacular about that? No, unless you insist on making something else of it, this piece is just about a simple quarryman who once lived in Needmore and smoked a large quantity of Granger. And about love.

Most of the years he spent in stone quarries, Jot operated a noisy, hot, smoking, Ingersol steam channeling machine. Unless you've seen one, or several of them, doing what they were built to do, this probably won't make much sense. A channeler looked like – well, an oversized, black hot water tank that stood upright on a rectangular chassis with two miniature railroad wheels front and back. A smokestack stuck out of its top, and a door at the bottom opened into a firebox from which the machine derived its locomotion and power.

Mounted on one side, and plainly visible to the operator, a tall diamond tipped steel plunger blade rose vertically. A channeler moved horizontally over small gauge tracks in runs from sixty to as many as two hundred feet. As it moved on its tracks, the vertical blade noisily pounded a two inch channel in the homogenous stone. It took three men to keep one going; the operator, a fireman, and a tender.

There is a black and white photograph of Jot on a channeling machine hanging from a wall at the Day and Carter Mortuary in Bedford. When we talked several years ago, Jot speculated that it is probably the only one of its kind. The black and rusting hulks of a couple such channelers are stored behind the chain link enclosure that surrounds the old school buildings on Hoosier Avenue, in Oolitic. They are mastodons of a past industrial age.

Recalling his years on them, Jot modestly observed, "It wasn't sich awful hard work, but it shook you around a little."

Most of his years were spent in the PM&B Quarry, south of Needmore and north of Oolitic. Until the Ruel W. Steele four-lane highway was built and old State Road 37 at that point reverted to its original owner, the Indiana Limestone Company, the quarry was visible to passersby on the old roadway.

Jot continued working there long after the channeling machines were replaced with more modern methods of removing stone from quarries, taking his retirement, finally, at age seventy-three. When I visited with him he was a tall, slim, handsome man of eighty-seven. He wore an old style navy cardigan over a light blue shirt opened at the collar, neatly pressed navy trousers, black socks and high-top black shoes.

Jot's people came from Diehl Holler, situated east of Oolitic, but he was born on a farm near Judah. He completed the six grades offered at McFadden School and, after trying his hand at several jobs, began life as a quarryman at age eighteen. After a few years, he decided he wanted to be a farmer. He and his wife, Sophia, packed their belongings into two wagons, along with their two sons, Murray and Wilford, and with two teams pulling, moved to Tunnelton.

"Took a whole day agoin' over there," Jot recalled.

While they were there Sophia gave birth to their only daughter, who later became Mrs. Thanna DePierre. Because he "didn't fancy farm life," Jot soon returned to Needmore, a trip that "took another day acomin' back," he said. Attempting to pinpoint the date of his return he smiled and said, "I can't remember no longer than my arm, anymore. But it's been a right smart awhile ago. I imagine it's been fifty years. Bound t'be."

Murray and Wilford played basketball at Needmore High School. Sophia, who died five years before this meeting, rarely saw them play because, she complained, the game was too rough to suit her. Her husband did not attend games because, "I never did think of basketball no more than nothin'," he said.

His dislike for the game, however, did not spill over to the kids who played it. Jot had an especially tender spot for kids. One of his four grandchildren, Beverly Wilson, said of him, "I never saw a child who didn't love him." His daughter, Thanna, remembered that, "We knew that love when he patted us on the back. He'd pat us on the back and we knew that love was there," she said.

Thanna recalled the special warmth he held for her because she was the only girl in the family, and the baby at that. "I always waited for him at the end of our lot at suppertime, when he'd come home from work," she remembered. "He'd come up the hill past Earl Turner's store, lunchbox aswingin'. And I'd be there because he always saved me something from his lunch. Maybe it would be a piece of cake he wouldn't eat for lunch, so that he would have it for me, or maybe a piece of pie. But there was always something for me in that lunchbox. And I was always there at the end of the lot, waiting for him to come home."

The recollection swept over her in a wave of emotion. Her throat constricted so that she was unable to talk. She looked at her father. From where I sat I could see that her eyes were iridescent with welling tears. Her whole face was alight with an inexpressible love for him. And Jot sat quietly, smiling at the memory of it all.

Thanna and her husband, Richard, and Murray and his wife, Thelma, and Wilford and his wife, Annetta, all lived close by. Ever since he'd been widowed, Jot had taken turns eating with them each night. Except Saturday, which was his day to fix his meals, "And that's generally a sandwich," he said.

Quarrying is a summertime job. Looking back on the days when he and Sophia had to keep their family in food, clothing and shelter in summer and winter on summertime wages, Jot commented, "We didn't have to have too much, and it didn't cost too much to get what we had to have."

Jot's full name was William Jot Diehl. In a moment of nostalgia, he revealed how he had come by his middle name. "I was named after an old storekeeper near Guthrie whose store was along the Monon Railroad tracks," he said. "He told my father that if he would name me after him, he'd give me a suit of clothes. Boy, he dressed me up like a doll. Jot Tincher was his name."

When Jot was not down at Earl Turner's puffing on a pipeful of Granger, or eating at the home of one of his children, he just might have been sitting on his small front porch. It was from the comfort of a swing, suspended from the porch ceiling by chains, that he would talk to a visitor, feed the birds, or pat the head of an old neighborhood dog named "Feller."

Yes, except that he worked in a stone quarry, there was nothing spectacular about Jot Diehl. Unless, of course, you do as I sometimes do: stop in Needmore at suppertime to watch him, lunchbox aswingin', come up the hill past Earl Turner's Store to a little girl awaiting him there.

74

THE RIGHT PLACE

Although severely injured and nearly killed by her "experience" of October 24, 1980, Wanda Johnson declared with a bright smile on her pretty face, "I was in the right place at the right time. Thank God!"

Except that she did some pre-Halloween shopping in the afternoon, that Friday had begun ordinarily enough. At Applacres, in Lawrence County, she had purchased caramel candies, cider and apples, for the season's trick-or-treaters. Later, in Bedford, nearer to her R. 1, Norman home, she had shopped in three grocery stores.

At home, later, she put away the perishables and left the Halloween things on the kitchen table. It was time to pick up her eleven year old son, Matt, at basketball practice at Heltonville School. Changing from a colorful crocheted poncho to a hooded sweater for the short trip, Wanda stood before a full-length mirror and buttoned it up, examining her appearance while doing so. That was the last she was to remember until the following Tuesday. Wanda had made a strange journey to what she later said was "The right place at the right time."

While driving her 1971 Monte Carlo on U.S. 50, three miles from home, an approaching Blazer went out of control and struck her head-on. With the aid of a power extricator, and with the help of Shawswick Township volunteer firemen, it took Bedford firemen an hour to free her from the wreckage. While she was trapped, Wanda apparently was conscious – rescuers reported she spoke with them while they worked.

At the Bedford Medical Center where she was taken by ambulance, Wanda's injuries were determined. She had a compound fracture of the left knee, her right knee was cut at the cap, her right arm and ankle were broken, she had a fractured rib, her spleen was severely damaged and she was bleeding internally. Her face and forehead were cut so badly some sixty stitches were required to close the wounds. It was feared that one facial injury would result in the loss of her right eye. Fortunately, it didn't. A doctor at the hospital commented that in another hour Wanda might have become a corpse. As it was, she remained in the hospital's intensive care unit for little more than a day. However, it was not until the next Tuesday that she knew where she was.

"When I realized where I was, and after I learned what had happened, I had a talk with God," Wanda said. "I told Him how happy I was that I had been alone at the time of the accident, and that Matt nor his father was with me."

Frank Johnson, unaware that his wife had been in a traffic accident, had seen the passing ambulance carrying Wanda to the hospital on his way home from his job in Bedford. Minutes later, he arrived at the scene of the wreck and recognized her Monte Carlo.

"I was the only one hurt," Wanda continued her recollection of her talk with God that Tuesday. "And I was so happy that I was I said, 'Thank you God!' "

A visitor who came to see her then interrupted that talk and stood in awe of a strangeness she said she felt in the room. "I can feel the presence of God in your room, Wanda," her visitor had said in breathless greeting.

"I know," Wanda had replied happily. "That's because He's here."

Wanda believed God came to her on two more occasions: November 24, when she said the rented hospital bed in her bedroom was bathed in a golden light; and on the following March 16, when she said God had encouraged her to stand on her healing legs.

"Therapy was the most difficult part of my recuperation," Wanda said of her effort toward walking again. Initial therapy was begun during the sixteen days of her hospitalization. After she was dismissed, it was continued at home with the aid of her sister, Peggy Kunkle, of Heltonville, who had moved in to help.

"But on March 16, God spoke to me and said, 'Wanda, you can stand up!' I had tried before, and I almost fell on my face each time. But after I heard Him, I clasped my hands in my lap and stood up. I sat down then, and then I stood up again. Then I just went up and down and up and down in that chair, and crying and crying and crying and saying, 'Thank you, Jesus! Thank you, Jesus!' I was just so thankful," she said beaming.

Wanda had been a church member for ten years. Her husband also attended church regularly. Matt, too, was a believer. But since Wanda's accident and her subsequent visits from God, their lives had changed.

"Everything is so beautiful now," Wanda tried to explain. "Ever since my natural father died, when I was six, there was a part of me that was always alone. Now my life is full. I never feel alone. And I'm constantly thanking God for everything," she said.

Church — everything — began to mean more to Wanda. She attributed the change to the accident, or "the experience," as she preferred to call it.

"If God were to come to me today and say He wanted to take me back to October 24, and have me leave the house just ten minutes later so that I could have avoided what really did happen, I would say, 'No,' " she said. "I would not trade the experience for anything. God allowed me to come back with a smile, and He has come to me. He has changed my life. There is no way that I'd want to change what has happened."

Wanda's legs were still not as strong as they needed to be at that time. She still had some difficulty climbing steps, but she worked at her therapy daily. "Nothing can stop me," she declared. "I will eventually whip this. All of it. Because God is with me."

She smiled knowingly, a beautiful smile in a pretty face that gave little or no indication of the painful physical experience of October 24, 1980.

Robert Hall, The Author, Paul "Punk" Love
The Three Fishermen

GOIN' FISHIN'

Although I am not a stranger to southern Indiana, were my life now to depend on it, I could not find my way back to Bat Hollow Lake. But I am not altogether certain that I should want to.

However, on that torrid summer afternoon, when we slipped away from the safety and comfort of the newspaper office and drove into lush, outdoors Indiana, I was as anxious to get there as were my two companions.

They had been there before, they said. Wild, they said. Too remote for most anglers, they said. The greatest panfish-hole around, they said. If the last were ever true, then I say now that it may still be, for we certainly did little that day to disrupt its pristine state. But hold on a second, while I begin at the beginning.

To repeat, there were three of us. Robert "Bob" Hall, Paul "Punk" Love, and I; a trio of small-town daily newspaper persons yoked with a ho-hum summer afternoon. We'd had them before, else why would we carry fishing gear at the ready in the trunks of our cars?

So, there we were, the three of us in one car, humming over sizzling blacktop county roads, bubbling with anticipation. Our destination, an aging WPA accomplishment of the mid-1930s called Bat Hollow Lake, situated in Hoosierland's scenic hills.

Stopping at last at the terminus of a dead-end gravel road, we gathered up our gear. Through three strands of rusty barbed wire fence we hunched, grunt, grunt, grunt. Into a density of knee-high undergrowth we struggled, puff, puff, puff. At some point during this tangled, sweaty travail, someone (if the other two of us ever find out who, we'll skin him alive) said, "Watch out for snakes."

That was the magic word. Snakes! The air suddenly wooshed from our ballooning expectations. The earlier hope of savory fillets for supper became a bitter taste in our mouths. We, who so anxiously had sought to escape the boredom of a dull office afternoon for a crack at a venerable fishing hole, were now nervously preoccupied with – SNAKES! Suddenly, each of us was secretly wishing he was back at his desk.

Yet, we continued our stumbling, cautious trek through the underbrush. While we were thus engaged, Bob, unsolicited and uninvited, took it upon himself to recount for Punk and me, a "true" experience with a copperhead, a pit viper endemic to our part of Indiana.

80

During Bob's recitation, the little hairs on the back of my neck bristled and stood straight out, in warning of impending agonizing death from snakebite. And wouldn't you know, when he was finished with that hair-raising tale, Punk felt compelled to relate in funereal tones a near-fatal encounter a friend had with a "really big" ophidian that had almost devoured his leg.

I could have told the snake story to end all snake stories; my mother once being frightened by a ten-inch green snake while picking dandelions in a meadow near our house. So terribly threatened had she been by that thing she threw down her basket and knife, hiked up her long skirts, and lit out for home, never once touching the ground on the way, her little boy right behind her. Then she ordered me back to the vacated field to retrieve the basket and knife. Don't think that wasn't a fearsome thing to do, facing that green monster all by myself.

Yes, I could have told that story. But, by the time those two guys had finished with their tales, our heads already were like a Gorgon's – a mass of writhing serpents – and we didn't need any more scary stuff.

We should have turned around right then and fled back to the newspaper office. But we didn't. With eyes focused on the thick undergrowth, we pushed on. Finally, wet with sweat and bloody from attacking briars, we climbed the last hurdle to our destination, a high levee that encloses Bat Hollow Lake. On the opposite side we skidded and bumped our way down a steep, red clover-covered incline to the narrow foot-path around the water's edge. Then the fit hit the proverbial shan.

We later were somehow able to piece together this much of what we think happened: As the three of us, in single-file, warily tippy-toed over imaginary crawling things along the narrow footpath, the flipping tip of someone's flyrod inadvertently touched the back of Bob's right leg.

With the loudest "WHEEE!" I'd ever heard, and one that must have startled every living thing in the countryside, he went into a sudden vertical thrust. Straight up, up, up, he went, shrieking, somewhere along the way, that awful word: "SNAKE!"

In compulsive reaction to that heart-stopping demonstration, Punk, for some reason he could not later explain, let go a loud "W-H-O-O-O-P!" And up he zoomed, to rendezvous with Bob.

I might have remained on the ground to do battle with the huge serpent myself, but I had no choice in the matter. During his takeoff, the tip of Punk's fishing rod had jabbed me just below and to the left of my right hip pocket. I kid you not, I was certain I'd been grasped you know where by an asp. Z-o-o-o-m! I was suddenly airborne with a clarion W-H-O-O-O-E-E-E!

There we were, WHEEE, WHOOOP and WHOOOEEE, in a holding pattern over the footpath. Blubbering like idiots about a big SNAKE that was lying in wait for the first of us to land somewhere amid the tangle of abandoned fishing gear on the footpath below, we stayed up there for as long as possible.

On the ground much later, huddling courageously back-to-back for protection, we continued our blubbering search for the slithery thing. It was to no avail. Slowly, thank Heaven, or we might still be out there, our hysteria subsided. A degree of sanity finally took hold of us, and we began boldly to assure and reassure ourselves that we had been duped by our own overworked imaginations. "Of course!" we said. "Right!" we agreed. "Exactly!" we chorused.

We bravely cowered there for – well, almost forever – praying for wings so that we might fly over the jungle of underbrush that separated us from our only transportation back to the safety of the newspaper office.

MCQUEARY'S CORNER

After the blizzard of 1977-78 and plows had opened a single snow-banked lane of blacktop roadway leading to it, I drove to Alvin and Ethel McQueary's store. A small, compact establishment, it sat in a sharp bend of the road in rural Brown County popularly known as McQueary's Corner. The winter storm had descended on southern Indiana on a Wednesday. It wasn't until the following Sunday night that the single lane on State Road 135 was opened, and McQueary's Corner could again be reached from the outside world. When I arrived Alvin and Ethel were still incredulous at the amount of snow that had fallen and drifted there.

"It's hard to believe," I remember her saying, "that we got this," and she raised her chin toward a window and the high snow drifts outside.

"We've seen bad drifts before," Alvin said of the snow covered corner and its history of severe winter snows of other years. "But we've never seen anything like this."

The storm struck in the first month of the McQueary's twenty-eighth year as Brown County storekeepers. They lived in a house that was within walking distance of the store and when the onslaught of the storm subsided they dug their way to the establishment. For four days afterward they kept it open to those residents who for miles around were caught short or completely without the daily necessities of life.

Displaying great strength and endurance, people began arriving at the store by late morning Thursday. They came on foot, down from the surrounding snow-covered hills and up from the wooded hollows. They struggled through huge drifts, some walking for miles to reach McQueary's Corner. One of two boys who had accompanied their father collapsed into a chair after reaching the safety and warmth of the store. "We'll never make it back home," he gasped. They did. They took to the fields on their return trip; the snow had not drifted as much there. Some who arrived at the store were overcome with fatigue and cold and were unable to speak until after considerable rest. They brought gunny sacks and pillow cases in which to carry their groceries. When they left the store for the return trip home they carried them slung over their shoulders.

By virtue of her position as lady storekeeper, where she daily heard news of people who lived for miles around the store, Ethel McQueary knew which families had babies and youngsters. She was able to share the store's supply of fresh and powdered milk proportionately with them, until it was gone. She did the same with eggs. When one weary slogger arrived too late to share in the store's supply, Ethel could not deny him. She walked the snow covered path to her own refrigerator and brought back six of her own family's ten eggs for the man.

After the Sunday night opening of one lane of State Road 135, milk and bread and egg deliveries began arriving at the small store. Isolated residents of the surrounding rural area found walking the plowed lane easier than struggling through the drifts. A few four-wheel drive vehicles began appearing, and their drivers were generous with rides for the walkers. A few more days and life around McQueary's Corner returned to normal.

A mid-April return there found the snow gone. In its place were colorful flowers, green grass, fruit tree blossoms, bloomed magnolia trees and green pines. But memories of winter still lingered.

"I can just close my eyes and see all of it again," Ethel said. "There's a lot of last winter left in my mind. I'll never forget it."

I recalled that the winter day I had arrived there it was rumored a man had died of exposure near Houston. Ethel said the report proved groundless. She added that another man who had lain out in that blizzard suffered frozen hands and feet, which later had to be amputated.

"When we have a beautiful day," she said, "we just naturally start talking about last winter. It seems that we appreciate more our ability to get out. The winter comes up, too, when one customer will see another in here and say something like, 'Well, I know it's spring, since you're out.' "

The McQueary's came to Indiana from their native Kentucky. They lived in Columbia, Kentucky, until the spring of 1950, when Alvin helped some relatives move to Indiana. Driving around in rural Brown County, he got lost and stopped at the store, which then was the Bill Smith Grocery Store, and asked directions out of there. He said something to Smith about Brown County being good looking country, and that he liked it. Smith told Alvin that it could all be his, for a price. That was Monday, April 30, 1950.

Alvin returned to Columbia where he told Ethel about what he'd found in Brown County, Indiana. Two days later they arrived at Smith's and purchased the corner lock, stock and sixty-acre farm that went with it.

"It's like the place we came from," Ethel said of the rural area. "I love it here." Their children, Linda, Marge, Leon, and Robert, shared in their parents' enjoyment of that place.

Alvin and Ethel bought additional ground until they owned a total of one hundred ninety-seven acres. Christmas trees covered several acres. Although much of the crop was marketed annually to wholesale buyers, scores of the trees were sold to individuals. Countless people in Brown and surrounding counties will remember McQueary's Corner as the place where they used to "chop down" the family Christmas tree.

THERE WAS A SPARK

The whole world seemed to rock and tremble at about ten minutes till four o'clock the afternoon of May 1, 1968, and a mushroom cloud, black and angry, rose high enough into the sky above tiny Helmsburg to be seen from as far away as Columbus. It was not an earthquake, as Verna Rushton, at her home a quarter mile away, had thought. It was an explosion. And it remains a wonder that it hadn't blown or burned the Brown County village off the map.

"We'd seen smoke earlier," Verna said. "Evelyn Cornelius had pointed it out and said, 'Something's burning.' I said, 'Oh, that's probably Buck Brummett burning his tires again.' Later, when the big explosion happened, it was just like an earthquake, the ground trembled so."

Verna and her husband, William (Rusty) Rushton, were at home at the time enjoying a break from Rushton's Super Service, the town's gasoline filling station. But Rushton's was more than an ordinary filling station of that period. From the time the couple had bought the place from Clyde Brown, four years earlier, they had been reinvesting every dime they earned in the business. A forerunner to convenience stores, Rushton's provided Helmsburg and surroundings, and passersby on State Road 45, complete filling station and auto repair services, auto parts and accessories, wrecker service, groceries, sporting goods, ammunition, fuel oil delivery and free coffee. In the four years that they had owned it, Rusty and Verna Rushton had more than doubled the station's annual gross, increasing it to six figures. "And we sold a lot of gasoline," Rusty Rushton said.

It was a delivery of gasoline that had precipitated the fire that caused the smoke seen by Evelyn and Verna, and caused the subsequent violent explosion. Wesley Eugene Steele, then forty-two, had driven a tanker loaded with seventy-five hundred gallons of gasoline onto the station's drive. After transferring a portion of the load into underground tanks, Steele backed the tanker to an above-ground thirty-five hundred gallon storage tank. A gravity flow conduit allowed the gasoline in that tank to be transferred into the station's underground tanks when they needed refilling.

To make the transfer into the above ground storage tank, Steele used an electrically operated portable pump. The only electricity available to operate it was from a receptacle in the station's large auto repair garage, and Steele had backed the tanker close enough to its open doors to make the connection. During the pumping process the garage filled with the pungent fumes of gasoline. Unknown to Steele at the time, a faulty hose connection was spewing raw gasoline over the drive. It wasn't until some time later, when station patron Oral Voland, then county surveyor, told Steele he smelled "a strong odor of gasoline" that the leak was discovered. Steele then made a common error, and, this time, a costly one. Instead of using the emergency switch to shut down the pump, he pulled the plug from the receptacle, interrupting the flow of electricity. There was a spark.

"That spark," recounted Chelsea Sisson, who worked in the Chitwood Hardware and Furniture Sales store across the highway from the filling station, "ignited the gasoline on the ground and the flames raced up the back of the truck to the station building."

Flames then ignited the fumes inside the forty by eighty foot adjacent garage and Helmsburg heard its first of several explosions that afternoon. Just that quickly Steele's clothing was ablaze. At the risk of their own lives, two bystanders, Ernie Pate and Rodney Southern, rushed to his aid. At the same time, Carolyn Southern, Rodney's wife and the Rushton's daughter, ran to a telephone and dialed the operator for the Nashville Fire Department, some seven miles distant. The telephone operator, Carolyn said, apparently misunderstood what she said and asked if she wanted to be connected to Nashville, Tennessee.

In the meantime, some fifty to sixty quart cans of oil in the garage began exploding. "They were going off like popcorn," said Verna Rushton. Firearms ammunition in a steel container was also exploding like gunshots. Pieces of burning rubber rained down on the roof of the hardware store. Flames engulfed a nearby sawmill owned by Ben George and Charles Richards. The fire jumped a gravel road and incinerated the home of Ruth Hamblin. It appeared that all of Helmsburg would go up in flames before someone finally got through to the nearest fire department, in Nashville, Indiana.

At long last the wail of sirens could be heard in the distance as fire trucks from Nashville, Fruitdale, Gatesville and Bloomington made their way to the scene. Following them were scores of curious people in automobiles and other vehicles. By this time, the center of Helmsburg had got so hot that, "When firemen sprayed water on the propane tanks at Chitwood's across the road, it sizzled," Rusty Rushton said.

Some people said the fire raged out of control for forty-five minutes before the above ground gasoline storage tank blew up. "I was up getting pieces of burning rubber off the roof of the hardware store when that thing blew," Sisson remembered. "The force of the explosion knocked me down and burned the side of my face."

Clarence Chitwood, co-owner of the hardware and furniture store with his wife, Goldie, was behind their establishment on another street near Long's Grocery, and the blast burned him. Goldie, who was in the hardware store at the time of the explosion, remembered that it broke out windows, "And it cooked the paint on the side of the store, damaged trees and scared us to death."

Bob and Libby Roudebush looked down on the fiery scene from a hillside a half-mile away. "Pieces of burning things landed in the field around us," Libby said of the force of the explosion.

While it may have seemed that hell itself was raining fire and brimstone down on Helmsburg, it was the awful explosion itself that snuffed out the fire and actually saved the community. It also left the above ground gasoline storage tank "mashed flatter than a fritter."

Steele, who was the only person seriously injured, survived. At some time during the fire, Rusty Rushton took enough smoke into his lungs to aggravate an asthmatic condition. Several buildings were damaged and three were totally destroyed. Damage was set at a hundred-thousand dollars.

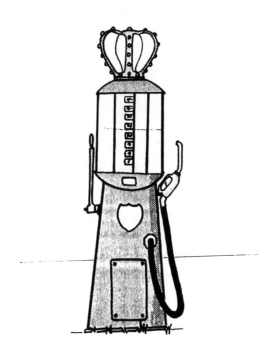

TONY CHAPMAN

Since I've been sitting here, Tony has shivered a few times. Each time I asked him if he were cold, and each time he shook his head from side to side. When I came into the ward and approached his bed he spoke one word, my name: "Larry," he said. Since then he's been trying to clear a congestion from his throat. He has asked twice for ice. Twice the nurse told him it was coming.

I'm writing this at his bedside. We are in Children's Hospital in Cincinnati, Ohio. This is an intensive care unit, and there are three other children who are being treated here besides Tony. In this ICU the nurses and patients are on what they call a one-to-one arrangement; a nurse, each of whom is an RN, to care for each of the four children.

Tony's nurse is busy with the paraphernalia of the sick that fills this ward. I am seated on a backless stool. Only members of the family are allowed here. That's what this nurse said when she saw me. "Only family – mother, father – you know." She added sincerely, "I'm sorry."

I looked at her nameplate: Rosemary Gibson, RN. Then I looked past her pink and white young face into her blue eyes. "I'm family," I said. Her eyes fell softly on Tony's dark skin, his black kinky hair against the hospital-white pillow slip under his head. She turned them toward me as a sudden flush rose to her cheeks. A little smile touched her lips. She shrugged her shoulders. I knew then that it would be all right to stay.

Tony weighs about sixty pounds now, a mere slip of the boy who was stricken last August and who has been seriously ill on and off since then. Under a patch-quilt his body seems very small. Yet, if he could stand, the top of his head would reach my shoulders. That's pretty tall for an eleven year old.

Tony has had a lobectomy of the left lung. A fungal pneumonia, slow in responding to medication, pushed its way into an artery and caused him to hemorrhage. There was no time to lose. The youngster was rushed to surgery where he remained for almost five hours, and where he left a portion of that lung. He was on life supports for about seven hours until, according to his physician, he made an amazing recovery and was able to sustain his frail body without assistance.

Tony has coughed up some thick yellow-green phlegm. Wiping his mouth with tissues, I've noticed the phlegm is streaked with blood. That's how they knew he was bleeding internally before he was rushed to surgery; he was coughing up blood. The appearance of it frightened me, and I called it to the attention of the nurse. I was told not to worry, that everything is all right, that it is not unusual for a person suffering from pneumonia to spit up blood.

Tony awakened briefly, "I want to go home," he whispered to me.

At home, in Bloomington, Indiana, Tony has a new bicycle, a BB-gun, and a pool table – gifts from readers of the newspaper I work for – and from his fifth grade classmates at Grandview School. In good health he'd be having fun with those gifts, but it may be days, weeks, before he can return to them.

He has the ice now, brought to him by Alton Kessinger, a Naval Reserve hospitalman third class who prefers to spend his drill weekends at this hospital, as do many other volunteers. "I'd rather do this than sit at the reserve center one weekend a month," he said. As he spoke, he fed the ice to Tony from a spoon. The ice makes crunching sounds between Tony's teeth.

The youngster is one of many children in the U.S. who have acute lymphoblastic leukemia. The disease is still in research, and in reputable hospital centers across the nation like this one, children, like Tony, lie waiting and hoping for a cure. Last summer, during school vacation, Tony had no warning that he would become sick with the disease, and that in just a few months he'd be looking for a miracle to restore his body to health. It had happened overnight. One day in early August he became ill and in a matter of hours he was in the hospital. He was later moved to this one for treatment of leukemia. He isn't the first child to be stricken in this manner, nor will he be the last.

The ice has made him cold, and he has asked me to pull the quilt up around his thin, ebony shoulders. He

94

shivers visibly. His physician, Gerald Vladimer, has told me that Tony is fast becoming the pet of the floor. He's been here for more than seven weeks, this trip, and almost everyone who works on this floor has come to know him. When he was taken to surgery some day-shift employees returned to the hospital that night to check on his condition, to help the nurses then on duty.

Vladimer, a pediatrician, is a fellow practicing under Dr. Beatrice Lampkin, chairman of this department, and Drs. K. Y. Wang and Ralph Gruppo. Vladimer wears his dark hair long, in the fashion of the day, and has a thick well-kept brown mustache. His collar is unbuttoned to reveal a turtle neck undergarment. He explains leukemia to me. His words and phrases are technical, cryptic. I don't understand. I am able to view Tony's illness only as a demon that defies the exorcism of research.

While he is speaking, a little black boy approaches Vladimer. There are tears in the child's eyes. His speech comes out of his mouth in a series of strange noises; no words. Spittle hangs in shiny strings from the corners of his mouth. Vladimer takes the child into his arms, embraces him as a father would embrace a son. He coos to him, pats him on the head, the shoulders, touches his lips to the little dark wet face. The child rests his head on the physician's shoulder, his face starkly black against the white of the lab coat. He is quiet. I feel a swelling in my throat – Vladimer is white; twenty-eight.

He expresses a hope that Tony can go home soon. "It is important, even in his condition, that he be returned to a normal life," he said. "It is also important that Tony is not judged by other children, or adults, in terms of the leukemia he has. He is no different from any other child. He needs to be allowed the

95

same considerations allowed any other child, including returning to school."

Tony's home is a gold and brown mobile home at Heatherwood Court, on the southwest side of Bloomington. It was there, while he was enjoying life as any normal, healthy boy enjoys life, with his mother, Hazel Chapman, his two sisters, Dorothy and Sharon, and with his neighborhood friends and schoolmates, that he was stricken. He was brought here for bone marrow transplants when he developed the infection in his lungs. It was a heartbreaking setback. His physician discussed the problem with him, "man to man," and told him how it would delay the transplants. He also told Tony that the medication to cure the infection would be something less than pleasant to take. The conversation at the time between Tony and the doctor and Tony's mother went like this:

Doctor: "This medicine, if you take it, will make you very ill. So ill that you're going to wish you were dead. Can you take it?"

Tony, looking up at his mother: "Mom, can you take it?"

Mrs. Chapman: "Yes, Tony. I can take it."

Tony, turning his eyes back to Dr. Vladimer: "Don't worry, doctor. We'll take it."

From Vladimer, as well as from nurses, particularly blonde, blue-eyed RN Donna McAffee, who was spokesperson for the rest of the nurses, I learned much about Mrs. Chapman. "I can't say enough about this woman," Vladimer told me. "She's been staying here with Tony. When the parents of these other children –" he gestured toward the twenty-four-bed division of hemo-oncology "– go home she takes over, walking the kids up and down the halls, carrying the little ones, answering their calls for assistance, for water, or whatever."

96

Vladimer said that Mrs. Chapman, during these last seven — almost eight — weeks while her son has been hospitalized here, has hardly slept. That among the patients and staff of the division she is becoming better known as "the ward mother" than by her own name. "She's always ready to help, and she gets along so well with all the patients," said nurse McAffee. "She looks after the little ones, especially. She's just been the best person. You don't see a lot of parents like her coming in here. We have a lot of respect for her."

Mrs. Chapman has remained inside, around the clock, each day. "As long as my son is here, I will stay here," she said. She rests in the division's waiting room when the ambulatory little patients will let her. When she can afford it, she eats in the hospital's cafeteria. Her two older children are staying with friends in Bloomington. I have received many letters at the newspaper from readers expressing their admiration for Mrs. Chapman.

Tony has become the most popular patient in the hospital. Many cards, letters and gifts have been arriving daily for him, many of them from other children. Patients and doctors and nurses, have asked me, "What kind of place is Bloomington, Indiana?" I have answered them all in the same manner. "Not only Bloomington," I told them. "Tony's friends come also from Spencer, Bloomfield, Smithville, Harrodsburg, Lawrence County, Brown County, Orange, Washington, Jackson, Morgan and other counties in Indiana. And from places beyond them." But the question is always put, "What kind of place is Bloomington, Indiana?"

Tony loaned me a few letters from children to run in this column for your pleasure. Here they are, beginning with one from Bloomington.

Dear Tony: You don't know me, so I will tell you about myself. My name is Jim Van Horn. If I met you,

I know I would like you. I go to Templeton School. I read about you in the newspaper. I know your wish to come home will come true and I hope you get your wish soon.

Dear Tony: I don't know you very well and you probably don't know me. My name is Larry Edward Knabel. Some kids call me King Edward The First, and I say that's right. Do not forget me, Tony. I'll have to say Good-Bye.

Dear Tony: I am in sixth grade at Cardinal Pacelli School. Get well soon. From Margaret Stenger.

Dear Tony: I've enclosed a card for you to give to your nurse friend, the one that's getting married. Our prayers are with you. Your friend, Betty.

Dear Tony: Hi, how are you? I am fine, my hobby is horses. My name is Charlie Matlock. I made a picture truck for you. I hope you like it. I am in the fourth grade. Your beloved friend, Charlie Matlock.

Dear Tony: Don't get a broken heart, we still care. Get well soon. Your friend, Mark Zando, (Cardinal Pacelli).

Dear Tony: My name is Tommy and I would like to tell you a poem. Roses are red, violets are blue, someone is special and that is you. Your friend, Tommy.

Dear Tony: My name is Gary, I am ten. I hope you get well. I hope you like my letter. I hope you can come to see us. I like math and IU. I like football and I like to read about wars. Your friend, Gary Whaley.

Dear Tony: I like you. I hope you get out of the hospital soon. You seem nice, what school do you go to? I wish you were going to our school. I think that you would be a nice friend. Would you be my friend if you would come to our school? I like baseball. I like to play tag. (This one had no signature.)

Dear Tony: I would like to be your friend. From Louis.

Dear Tony: I like to play cops and robbers, do you? I hope you will get well soon. Your friend, Tim.

Dear Tony: My name is Ricky. I hope you get to go home from the hospital. I wish you best wishes. I hope you can walk again and get over your disease. Your new friend, Ricky Abbitt.

Dear Tony: I am a girl. I know your mom. My name is Jackie Smith. I read in the newspaper about you. Our family is going to give your family some food. I hope you get well. Just hang in there. Get well soon. Your friend, Jackie Smith.

Dear Tony: I hope you get well fast. I think I would like you. It is going to be summer soon. Love, Frankie McGill.

Dear Tony: I hope you get better. Then you can go back to school and play with your friends. I like to play football and baseball. From Robert Webb.

Dear Tony: Here is a joke. What is the difference between a teacher and a train? The teacher says spit out the gum and the train says chew-chew. Hope you feel better. From Susan Graves, (Cardinal Pacelli).

Calling Tony: We still care about you even if you haven't met us. Your friend, Mike Finn, Cincinnati.

Tony: I hope you're feeling better. Do you live in a big family. I do. I live in a family of twelve. I have seven sisters and two other brothers and parents. Is the hospital nice? Have you met any kids in the hospital. Well, I hope so. From Libby Crane.

From a youngster who apparently has been hanging around an older crowd came this query: Dear Tony: Well how the hell are you . . . ?

One rainy Saturday afternoon two youngsters arrived at the cubby-hole that is my office at the newspaper. They carried with them a couple of glass jars filled with money they and some little friends had collected for Tony.

99

"You collected this from door to door in this rain?" I asked incredulously.

The little girl – she is ten – smiled. "Yes," she said.

"Gee," I said, "I don't know how to thank you."

She replied with the wisdom of the ages: "You just say 'thank you', that's all."

That, then, is the message of this column. Thank you. From Tony's bedside, thank you. You have done much. So much that the disbelieving mother of another young patient should exclaim, "I never knew there were people in this world like those in Bloomington, Indiana."

From the onset of his trial you have been giving Tony the will to live, to slow the dogged leukemia that weakens him. In his happiness he is aware of the miraculous healing of goodness. That awareness now is torn asunder by the nausea that apparently precedes internal and external hemorrhaging. The precious memory of that goodness is burned out of his body by a raging temperature and searing pain from an old surgery that will not heal.

Because you have been so kind to him, and because you have in your kindness become a part of him, you should know that his condition has been better. You should know, too, that Tony does not weep for himself, and because he doesn't, you should not weep for him. Pray for him, that is his wish, the wish of his mother, his sisters, his doctors and nurses. Continue remembering him with cards, letters and gifts and, yes, with the understanding empathy you must feel for him. Do not pity him, for Tony's courage is of noble origin, where pity could not thrive and cannot now take root.

If you can, remember the good times – the joy you took from making him a funky T-shirt, the fun you had putting together and wrapping a package for

100

him, the special feeling you put into the cards you made for him at school, and all the wonderful words you wrote on them, the satisfaction you got from sending the dollars to pay for food for his courageous mother, and his sisters, and the so many good things you've done for Tony and his family. Remember those times, and take joy from them. Remember, too, that Tony's needs, the needs of his family, are only beginning.

While here, I was introduced to Ray Speelman, a patient from Greenfield, Ohio, who is one of Tony's friends on this ward. Ray is one of two youngsters who benefited from a successful blood donor drive held in Bloomington. Until so many kind people donated blood in response to a plea for blood for Tony and others here, Ray's parents were saddled with a more than five-hundred dollar blood debt they were unable to pay. Ray asked me to take his thanks to you when I leave. To understand the depth of his appreciation you'd have to look into his large eyes.

It is time now for Tony to go to X-ray. They place him in a cart-like wheel chair. I whisper in his ear, brush his shiny black cheek with my lips. He nods his head; they move him away. I look up to keep the gathering moisture in my eyes from spilling down my face. For the first time I see pasted to the ceiling above each of the four beds in this ICU a colorful paper animal cutout. Above Tony's bed there is a yellow bear – a smiling yellow bear.

* * * *

Incredibly, Tony Chapman's condition improved. Early in April, Dr. Yong announced that Tony's leukemia was diagnosed under control, that it was in remission. It was great news for Tony, for his mother and sisters, for his many friends. He was released from the hospital and returned to his home on Good

101

Friday. But the child was far from total recovery. Yet, it was expected that with good food he would add pounds to his tiny frame and gain needed strength. To accomplish this, and to maintain his state of remission, he had to return to Children's Hospital as an outpatient for weekly medication.

There was pleasure in the returnings, for each visit was an opportunity to renew friendships with those youngsters whom he had left behind. Those trips also saddened him. They brought back memories of Allen, Ray, Michael, Angie, John, and Matthew, who, during his long stay there, had left Ward 4-West at Children's Hospital, in Cincinnati, "for the Ward 4-West in Heaven." Tony wept for each of them for "passing" (his metaphor for death), and for himself, because, he told me one day, death frightened him to a point beyond his ability to tell.

Weeks and months went by and Tony's condition seemed always in the balance. Yet it was a good time for him. His star had climbed and glowed brightly from a surprising height. During that period, doctors' orders were that he should be allowed to do anything he wanted, to eat anything he desired, and to go anywhere he could afford to go. Tony complied wholeheartedly. He did his utmost to live a fun life, enjoying everything, especially being out of the hospital and on his own two feet. Then one day Tony's high-riding star plunged downward. He was again admitted to Children's Hospital, in serious condition.

A column I wrote about this sad turn in Tony's life, and his need for more blood, evoked several letters to my editor that appeared in our newspaper. One, signed by three prisoners at the Indiana State Reformatory, appeared in the paper July 23, 1976. In part it read, "With heartfelt compassion, we read about little Tony Chapman, victim of leukemia, who is now in the

Children's Hospital, in Cincinnati, Ohio. There in the ward, seeing the deaths of his young friends, Tony naturally fears the future, where hope is troubled by doubt. Yet that little guy stands strong, not stumbling under the heavy burden that he carries.

"The prayers requested by his mother, we freely give, because God does answer prayers, and we know that in Him there is nothing impossible . . . We extend our hand of strength to Tony by offering him our blood . . . There are only three of us who are writing this letter, but there are other inmates in here who feel as we do, (and) can donate three or four hundred pints of blood to Tony now, and more in the future as it is needed. Our prayer is that the blood we give for Tony will be the buffering wind that turns the tide for him. If through our aid, his life is extended for one year, one month or even for one day, then it will be worth-while."

Tony knew that he was in relapse and seriously ill. But he preferred being at home. Physicians at Children's also wanted him to be at home, if he so desired, and they wanted him to enjoy every second of the life that was his to live. So he was allowed to go home. Soon his condition worsened, and on September 9, 1976, I had to write a story I had been dreading to put down on paper. It follows:

Tony Chapman is dead.

The frail boy who struggled so valiantly to live these past two years died peacefully at his home at five minutes before five o'clock this morning.

His death marks the end of a long, painful battle with leukemia. Stricken August 3, 1974, the youngster was reported near death several times, but he somehow managed to rally each time, surprising his physicians at Children's Hospital in Cincinnati, and sending a new thrill of hope through his family, and his many friends and well-wishers back home. But the disease slowly, relentlessly took its toll, and Tony's strength, his ability – even his desire – to fight back, weakened with each new onslaught.

What was to be his final struggle surfaced on Sunday, while he was attending church services. Under siege during previous attacks, Tony himself would announce that he was going back to Children's Hospital for treatment, and would direct preparations for the long car trip to Cincinnati. This time his mother began making plans to return there, but he told her, "I want to stay home." With a sinking heart, Hazel Chapman knew then that her son could fight no more.

In the meantime, Mrs. Patricia Hague of Dayton, Ohio, the mother of one of Tony's friends from Ward 4-West at Children's who had also died of leukemia, arrived at the Chapman home to help care for Tony. At four o'clock this morning, Bud and Wanda Baker and Mrs. Darlene Cochran, all parents of other Ward 4-West friends of Tony's who also died of leukemia, arrived from Covington, Kentucky, to help Tony's family with his care.

About five minutes before five o'clock, Tony asked for a drink of water. He drank thirstily, for a lengthy fever had dehydrated his body. Then he turned his face to his mother, taking her hands in his.

"I love you," she smiled down at him.

"I love you, too, Mama," Tony replied, and he closed his eyes.

As the first gray light of day paled the windows of the Chapman living room, Tony, just ten days short of his thirteenth birthday, was carried away from his home for the last time.

* * * *

Three days later I prepared the following for our editorial page:

The life of Tony Chapman was brief, but not so brief that it did not touch the lives of countless persons in his hometown of Bloomington, in cities and towns in Indiana, in the city of Cincinnati, in Illinois; Arkansas; California; Florida, and in other states, cities and towns in the U.S.

It would almost seem that his life, and his death at age twelve, were directed for divine purpose. Stricken with leukemia two years ago, the child's courage during the long, painful illness, his determination to live – to live happily and without complaint – inspired, warmed and encouraged those who came to know him.

"If Tony can be brave," an afflicted adult murmured of him one day, "I can, too."

"The kid's got guts," a laborer said after reading about one of Tony's several returns to Children's Hospital in Cincinnati. "He sure is teaching me a lesson."

One may only guess at the nature of that lesson, but perhaps a white minister speaking at the loveable little black boy's funeral Saturday, gave that lesson an interpretation.

"For a little while we forgot ourselves," he said. "For a little while we forgot our prejudices. We are all better people because Tony Chapman lived. He was more than just a friend, he was my brother."

This, then, was the impact of Tony Chapman's brief life. Because of him – his life, his illness – we were able to see beyond ourselves, beyond our personal needs. We saw so clearly that at his passing last Thursday tears of sorrow shut down a Bloomington plant's assembly line, and still other tears of sorrow were shed in other places at the news of his death.

Indeed, Tony Chapman took away with him when he died something of each of us who came to know him. But Tony Chapman left behind something that need never be lost – the ability to forget ourselves, and our prejudices, and the knowledge that we can be a brotherhood of better people, if we so desire.

Yes, the life of Tony Chapman was brief, but the truly significant messages of history have all been brief – so that they might better be remembered. – LInc.

* * * *

I often think of Tony, as I do my children who have died. A photo of him is tucked in the frame of a large Josef Israel print of children at some foreign, sandy shore – with pictures of kids and grandkids – that hangs in our family room. On a shelf in my den is a Timex wristwatch he gave to me as a gift a long time ago. It didn't work then and it doesn't work now. Suspended from a rawhide thong on the wall over the head of the bed in our master bedroom is a small wooden cross Tony carved and gave to me as a memento of our friendship. Across the face of the cross he printed in capital letters the word "LOVE." In a shoe box of sentimentalities I keep under my bed is the following note he left me. I want to share it with you.

"I know a man who writes a column in our daily paper. His name is Larry Incollingo. He is a good friend of mine. He has done many things for us. When I was sick he drove straight to the hospital, walked through the hall and stepped into my room.

"Boy was I surprised! It was good to see him. We talked about how thin I was getting. The people from Bloomington were always sending money and gifts with him. Being sick has not been fun, but because of him I have met so many nice people and have lots of new friends.

"He has written many articles about me, even had my picture in the paper. Sometimes when I go to town people will say, are you Tony Chapman? I guess this is a hard way to get famous. HA! HA! HA!"

It is signed, "Love, Tony Chapman."

THE LIBRARIAN

She warned me to "Be careful what you write about me. Don't make me look countryfied." I promised. Still, her beauty could not be separated from her countryfied speech or her countryfied ways. Yet, I promised. And I'll try to do as she requested.

She remembered that there were nine girls and one boy in her high school graduating class. "Sure I remember them," she said. "One of them called me from Loogootee this morning and we talked for over an hour."

She thought a few seconds. Then she began naming the female members of that old class: "There were Mara Freeman, she's dead now; Lois Marshall, she lives in Indianapolis; Pearl Renneker, she's dead; Belle Purhiser, she's also dead, and she left a large family who are still around here." She arched her brows thoughtfully. "How many is that now, four? Let's see. There was Eva Queen; Rosabelle Neighbors, she lives right back here; Gladys Hall, she's dead, too, and when she was alive she lived out here in the country. They all came in to school from the country." She paused. "I'm not going to forget any, am I? Oh yes, Iva Gaddis. Iva is alive. She's in a nursing home in Washington. How many is that?"

"Eight." I had been keeping count.

Not quite enough.

"Well, let's see," she mused. "Count them again." She repeated the names one by one, lingering on each while holding up a different finger for each. Reaching eight again she hesitated, then suddenly exclaimed, "And Marie Sides! Me! That's me!" She burst into laughter. "Most everybody calls me Marie Brown. It was Sides then. Marie Sides."

Marie Sides Brown was one of the elite few who spent all their school years in the same building in Shoals, a big red brick that later became a museum. She advanced from the first grade through high school without ever having attended a single class in another school building. It was a school where the rooms remained the same, where teachers, unless they got pregnant or died or retired, rarely changed, and where every day big kids helped care for the little ones.

There were no cars then and students came to school in town from the country on horseback, or in buggies. Some stayed in town all week, boarding with relatives or other families. Their parents drove in Friday to take them home for the weekend.

"We were country people," Mrs. Brown said. "And Shoals was a country town. Everybody came to trade here Saturday from Lost River, Mitchelltree, Halbert and Center townships."

They came to shop in East Shoals, on the east side of the East Fork of White River, whose muddy waters slice this Martin County town in two. The county courthouse and jail are in West Shoals, across the river, and visitors are dismayed because there isn't a public square full of stores around it. There's a walkway across the bridge. When I asked Marie Sides Brown why anyone should want to *walk* across the bridge she informed me through another burst of laughter, "To get on the other side."

Hearing her name in this Martin County seat, folks would point in the direction of the public library. Marie Sides Brown had served as librarian there ever since – well, our visit took place one cold November day in 1976 – fifty-six years earlier; ever since the passing of her husband, Roy Brown, in 1918.

"He'd been building an Army barracks down at Fort Knox, Kentucky, and took the flu and came home and died," she said. "It was terrible. He died in just a few days. You couldn't get a doctor, hardly, and then if you got one they didn't know anything about the flu. It was like this flu going around now is going to be. I haven't got my shot, but then my daughter doesn't want me to get one. A lot of people died from the flu in the 1918 epidemic. In a lot of families a mother and children died. Didn't anyone visit, it was so contagious, except to help with the sick. They shut down the school to try to stop the spread of it. There were no public funerals, and every week we'd read about who died in the newspaper. People were scared. It was awful. So many died. That's what makes people so scared about this one that's coming."

Marie Sides Brown had been a widow since that awful time, sharing her life with her daughter, Margaret Elizabeth. "They can't tell me that two families can't live together in the same house," the librarian said. "They can so, and it doesn't take much trying either. Once there were four generations living in our house." She recounted such an arrangement, a time during which she lived with her daughter, her parents, and their parents.

Shoals is a small enough town in which almost everybody knows almost everybody else. Like kids in most places, Shoals kids made noise in the library. "But," Marie Sides Brown hurried to say, "they don't make too much noise. And there's no use to be cross with them. You can't change people. Besides that, you get more out of them – most of the time – by being nice to them. If you just don't pay any attention to them, their noise doesn't sound too bad."

Of being a small town librarian, she said, "It's not a bad life." To support that view she added, "And Della Strange, the girl who was here before me, she's still alive."

AN UNUSUAL MAN

I wonder if Charlie Mayrose is in Heaven today. He wanted so badly to be wanted there before he left this life. He used to say, "I want nothing to stand between me and my good Lord. I love my Lord."

In his last years, Charlie worried that the gates up there would be closed to him unless all of his earthly debts were paid. They were, except for one, or so he thought. And, at an advanced age, he traveled from his home in Worthington, in Greene County, to Brazil, in Clay County, to repay that one – a debt that had been haunting him for forty-six years.

"The Bible says owe no man anything. Make restitution. And if I am to obey the scriptures, then I must pay what I owe," Charlie told me one day. "That's what I'm gonna do, too, soon as I find out how to go about it. I've got to get that done before I die."

Charlie explained that he incurred the debt when he and his family lived in Washington Township in Clay County. His three sons and three daughters were still mere children when a crippling carbuncle on the back of his neck left him unable to work.

"We lived near Bowling Green," Charlie gave the old homeplace a clearer reference point. "It was a jungle then. The mortgage payments on that piece of

111

land was acomin' due all the time and I was so sick and burnin' up with that thing on the back of my neck, I couldn't work. The little boys got behind the plow and got out the crop that year. Don't see how those little fellers did it. We got a crop, but it wasn't saleable.

"We had a trustee then by the name of Frank Morton," he continued. "He was a good man. An old man. He helped me. Every week he gave me a slip of paper that was good for five dollars worth of food or clothes at the store. Every week for twelve, maybe fourteen months. It seems like five dollars was a lot of money back then. Anyway, we did a lot with it. There were the six children, and my wife and me made eight, and that five dollars would see us through. I feel I owe that money to someone and I want to pay it back, now that I can. Before I die I gotta pay that. Owe no man nothing. That's what the Bible says."

Charlie seemed obsessed with the notion that time was fast running out on him. Yet it was a spry old man who climbed on furniture to take down photographs of his family so that I might see them close-up. He identified the image on each with an excitement that belied his advanced years. His blue eyes danced and his recollection was sharp.

Slight of build, the backs of his hands sticking out of the sleeves of a flannel shirt he wore were bony and red, and ridged with large purple veins. He said funny things that made me laugh, and serious things, which also made me laugh because of the way he said them. For such a small man Charlie had enormous ears that stood out prominently from his head, the left more than the right. They made me laugh, too. Not because I thought they were funny, but because they were Charlie's ears, and because, as I explained to him, my mother used to say my ears were over-sized and that she fully expected me to fly away

112

someday. That day with Charlie was one of the few times I could really laugh at my own self-consciousness about my ears. He seemed to understand what I was saying when I told him as much and he nodded his head and laughed with me. It seemed to me a moment of deliverance for the both of us. You would have had to have met Charlie, and seen me when I was a kid, to understand.

In a weaker moment, Charlie had expressed the lament of many older people when he complained, "I get so cold anymore. I've got on a heavy Union Suit, two pairs of pants, this heavy shirt, and I still get cold. And there's nights when I feel like I'll never see the morning. You see, don't you, why I gotta get that debt paid?"

It took only a couple of telephone calls to arrange for Charlie to repay the debt he believed he owed. And one day he walked into Clay County Auditor Margaret Butt's office, in Brazil, to do that. He returned two-hundred and sixty dollars, the amount they had agreed he received in poor relief so many years earlier. Mrs. Butt could find no Washington Township record to support Charlie's claim that he had been given that much money, or any money, for that matter. But Charlie insisted that in the 1920's he and his wife, Mary Margaret, and their six children, had received five dollars a week from the township trustee for at least one year. And, after overcoming the disappointment he expressed at having found a female and not a male auditor in the courthouse, Charlie, at eighty-seven years of age, wrote a check for the full amount and handed it to Mrs. Butt.

"The Bible says owe no man, and I don't want to die without paying my debts," he told her. Charlie was presented photostatic copies of the check and a receipt, by Mrs. Butt, which he later proudly displayed in his mobile home in Worthington.

"It was an unusual thing," Mrs. Butt said of Charlie's action. "He didn't owe anything. It really wasn't a debt. Poor relief is given and forgotten about. But he believed it was a debt. If everyone believed as Charlie, poor relief wouldn't be a burden to taxpayers. We are happy that he repaid the money, but I think we are more happy for him than we are for ourselves."

Repayment of the money gave Charlie a great sense of relief and pleasure. He often expressed himself in these words: "I'm sure happy I was able to give that money back. I sure am that," he would say.

Charlie lived much longer than he expected. Shortly before his death in Greene County Hospital, he took up residence in a nursing home. All the time he was there he pined for his mobile home, and his pets there, a long-haired black and white cat named Baby Boy, and a large black cat with no name, and his family photographs. Some people say that Charlie died of a broken heart. But his final illness, it was reported, was a stroke. Whatever it was, Charlie expected it. When a relative prepared to end a visit with him just before he died, Charlie said, "I hate to see you go." And he wept.

Charlie Mayrose was buried in Ashboro Cemetery, in Clay County, next to Mary Margaret, who died in 1954. He had lived ninety-five years "Loving the Lord" and removing all the obstacles he could think of that might have stood between himself and the Lord he loved. I wonder if he is in Heaven today?

THE ARCHER GANG

The Archer men, Thomas, Martin, and John, tensed with expectation at the ear-shattering banging on their cellblock door. It was about time, they thought. They'd been arrested and jailed in December. It was now three months later, the night of March 9, 1886, and their gang was just now breaking them out of the Martin County jail in Shoals.

For some time, the three had been listening to the stealthy approach of nighttime visitors. They also had heard the sounds of a struggle beyond the solid metal cellblock door while Sheriff John A. Padgett was overpowered and bound. Now they waited impatiently for the cellblock door to fall before the battering of a sledge hammer. After three months of confinement, the Archers, "Men of the country and of unrestricted ways," as one newspaper of the time described them, were ready to be set free. While they waited with bated breath, they savored visions of freedom that the racket conjured up in their minds.

At last the cellblock door fell from the fist-like grip of steel hinges, and, for a single exhilarating moment, the three prisoners luxuriated in the release for which they'd waited so long. Then their faces suddenly blanched with new and awful understanding. The

Archer Gang numbered a handful of men; these nocturnal callers were one hundred strong. Besides that, the Archer Gang never hid behind masks of any kind. These jail crashers wore white pillow slips over their heads. Then horror struck with the suddenness of a lightning bolt. These were vigilantes, and vigilantes could mean only one thing – a lynching!

Eyes wide with the sudden understanding of what awaited them, Thomas, Martin and John Archer cringed fearfully in their individual cells while the door locks were picked with shoe-button hooks. They pressed into corners, trying in vain to escape the long, gooseneck iron rods stuck through the bars, prodding, pushing, turning until the goose-necks could be secured to their limbs. Thus trapped, the Archer men were pulled up to the steel bars and held there, until some hooded intruders could enter their cells and bind them.

It was not so easy a task. The three Archers, two brothers, and the son of one of them, fought with the fury of cornered beasts, until they were broken and bloodied. Finally, their arms bound behind their backs with strips of muslin, the prisoners were half-led, half-dragged from the red brick jailhouse to two maple trees that to this day still shade the lawn of the Martin County Courthouse.

Leaders of a gang of criminals who for ten years had terrorized farmers in the Lost River Valley of Martin and Orange counties, the Archers could see the nooses awaiting them in the darkness. Thomas Archer, sixty, was led to the nearest tree from which a rope dangled with ominous finality. He was a tall man, and his executioners had failed to hoist his body sufficiently high enough; a foot dragged the ground and its carpet slipper, still warm from the ardor of life, came loose and fell to one side.

Petrified with fear, Thomas Archer's son, John, age thirty-three, and Thomas Archer's brother, Martin, age forty-five, both about to die themselves, had witnessed the lynching of the older man. For some reason that has escaped history, the hooded vigilantes who began the horror of that night by hanging the eldest Archer first, would end it by executing the youngest last. Thus it was that Martin Archer was chosen next to die. The acknowledged chief of the notorious Archer Gang, he was said to have been a man of intelligence, but cunning and full of deceit. It is recorded that he and his brother, who, before his eyes then was kicking into eternity at the end of a rope, had come up from Kentucky and settled in Lost River Township, where they subsequently had gathered around them a gang of outlaws. Minutes after witnessing the horrifying execution of his brother, Martin Archer was hanged from the second maple tree, facing the courthouse door.

John Archer had deserted his wife and had been living with another woman at the time of his arrest. He was taken into custody by a posse led by Sheriff Padgett after a chase that lasted an entire stormy December night. While he was living with his mistress, young Archer's wife and children became destitute and were given refuge at the county poor farm. It was she who set the wheels of justice turning in the direction of the Archer Gang. To Martin County Prosecutor Hiram McCormick, she gave a statement implicating Thomas, Martin, and John Archer, and a fourth man John Lynch, in the murder of a man of dubious character named Samuel A. Bunch.

This was not the only crime for which the three were punished. Nelson Spaulding, a wealthy farmer, had been cruelly hanged by the neck until he disclosed the hiding place of sixteen hundred dollars to a gang of rowdies believed to be the Archer Gang. He died a few days later. Other crimes attributed to the gang included similar torturings of other farmers.

117

During one of these later attacks on a private home, another man died.

People lived in fear of the notorious Archers, for gang members often let it be known that special atrocities awaited anyone fool enough to testify against them. But the woman scorned had no fear of them. From the statement given by John Archer's wife, it was learned that the gang had murdered Samuel A. Bunch on July 13, 1882, in a cave in French Lick Township. His body was found in a cavern there that had once been a commercial source of sodium nitrate, and was known as Saltpeter Cave. After the discovery of Bunch's remains there, it became more popularly known as Bunch Cave.

At trial, gang member John Lynch, who was taken into custody with the three Archer men, turned state's evidence. He supported John Archer's wife's statement with an eyewitness account of Bunch's death, which not only was a confession of his guilt but also implicated a fourth Archer in the death of Bunch; Samuel Archer, age twenty-eight.

While John Archer watched his father and his uncle hanged from the maple trees, awaiting himself the last of the tightening nooses that would strangle him to death on one of the trees, Lynch was safe in the Daviess County jail in Washington. He had told an incredible story to authorities there.

Samuel A. Bunch, who was forty-five at the time of his death, was said to have been the first leader of the gang that eventually became known as the Archer Gang. According to Lynch, Bunch and Samuel Marley, age twenty-two, and Martin Archer's son, "Mart," age eighteen, together stole a quantity of sawed logs and rafted them down-river to a secluded place in Illinois. There they left them tied together in a bend of the river and returned home where they planned to stay temporarily to avert suspicion.

While at home, young Mart became ill. While he was indisposed, Marley and Bunch sold the logs, keeping the money for themselves. Learning of this after recovering from his illness, Mart Archer demanded his share, threatening to expose Marley and Bunch. That Marley and young Mart were first cousins did not deter the young man, nor did the close relationship restrain Marley from what he was to do. Having already spent the money from the stolen logs, Marley and Bunch could not share it with Mart. Because they feared exposure and did not want to go to jail, they conspired against young Mart and drew straws to decide which of them should silence him. Marley drew the short straw. In due time, Mart was found shot to death on a lonely stretch of road leading to the Archer settlement in Orange County, near the Martin County line. The Archers immediately suspected Marley and Bunch, especially Marley, who had disappeared after the shooting.

The gang was called together. Bunch was seized, and accused of complicity in Mart's death. Bunch, according to Lynch, laughed in their faces. "I gave Marley the pistol to do the shooting, and I gave him a twenty dollar gold piece to get away, and I would do it again," Bunch is reported as having said.

Bunch was bound and taken to Saltpeter Cave, two miles distant. Standing in a semi-circle facing him were Martin Archer, Thomas Archer, John Archer, Sam Archer and, according to his testimony, John Lynch. Martin Archer threatened Bunch with death if he refused to disclose Marley's whereabouts, Lynch told authorities. Bunch is said to have laughed, "You don't have the guts to kill me."

Bunch reportedly had left his native Tennessee after killing a man. He later arrived in the Lost River Valley community west of Shoals, living across a ravine from Thomas Archer in what then was known and feared as the Archer neighborhood. As the original leader of the gang, Bunch had more than once displayed nerve and daring. Now Bunch had pushed those two assets to the limit. Lynch recounted that Martin Archer then turned to the other members of the gang and said, "If he doesn't tell, when I give the word, shoot! Any one of you who doesn't shoot will be shot."

The small cave room became deathly silent. Drab, tomb-like stone walls weighed heavily on the urgency of the ticking seconds of a life in the balance. According to Lynch, if Bunch was aware of his precarious position, he showed no sign of it. Given still another opportunity to speak, he refused. The members of the gang he once led, by then obedient to Martin Archer, and concerned with their self-preservation – for they knew that Martin Archer was capable of killing them, and even moreso since his son and namesake had been murdered – allegedly fired their guns into Bunch's body; five shots, almost as one. As though that were not enough, the men fired again into Bunch's body. Perhaps in the grip of anger, or a satanic need to continue their killing even past death, the gang fired still another round into Bunch's body.

Martin Archer then stepped forward. Placing his pistol against Bunch's head, he fired one last shot, a final vent to his agony and anger at the loss of young Mart. Then, true to his promise, Martin Archer examined each gun, Lynch told his incredulous listeners in Washington, to make certain that each man had fired as ordered. The gang left Saltpeter Cave, each of them going to his respective home, leaving the dead Bunch where he lay.

When Bunch came up missing, the Archers and Lynch immediately became suspect and were arrested. Because of a lack of evidence, they were released. A few weeks later, the killers of Bunch again gathered in the Saltpeter Cave. By this time Bunch's body was decomposed. They slipped what was left of it onto a plank, saturated it with kerosene, then carried it to a large pile of brush that had been cut and stacked for use as a pyre. A blazing fire did its work well, but not well enough. Large bones remained in its ashes and had to be buried. A hole was dug, the bones placed in it and covered with dirt, and a large tree was felled over the site, hiding the evidence. Their work well done, or so they believed, and filled with whiskey they had gulped from a jug carried to the cave with the can of kerosene, the gang members went home.

Lynch's story was hard to believe. He was requested to lead officials to Saltpeter Cave, and to show them where Bunch's remains were buried. Lynch had not lied about the burial; sure enough, large human bones were uncovered, as were several buttons that were identified as having come off Bunch's clothing. Lynch then aided authorities in locating Sam Archer.

Sam Archer had skipped bond August, 1885, after he was arrested for stealing cattle. By using fraudulent means, his father, Thomas Archer, obtained his son's release by bonding non-existent property. The younger man's promise to remain in the county proved worthless as the straw bond provided by his father. Lynch obtained, by deceit, for authorities, Sam Archer's whereabouts from Lynch's sister, who was Sam Archer's sweetheart.

After Sam Archer was arrested, he and Lynch were taken for safekeeping to the reformatory at Jeffersonville. But Lynch's confession leaked out. And piece by piece it was put together by the people who for years had been ravaged by the Archer Gang, and those pieces culminated in the depravity at Shoals by the hooded mob.

While Lynch and Sam Archer were safe in Jeffersonville, the last of the trio taken by force from the Martin County jail was murdered by the vigilantes.

John Archer, no braver than his father, or his uncle, both of whom had strangled to death before his eyes, was dragged screaming to the second maple tree where a dangling rope had awaited so long, and he was hanged.

When daylight came on March 10, the residents of Shoals were unprepared for what they saw suspended from the maple trees on the courthouse lawn. The vigilantes, as though to intimidate every transgressor, however vindicable, had left the bodies of the three Archer men hanging from the trees. A hush swept the town. Before long hundreds of people from everywhere, drawn by the horror of what had happened, came quietly to mill about the maple trees. They spoke in whispers as they viewed the blackened, oxygen-starved faces that were frozen in death above the stiffened ropes around their necks. The lifeless bodies hung there until late in the afternoon when the sheriff cut them down and released them to relatives.

They had brought coffins – pine boxes – and the dead were placed in them and loaded on wagons. In procession, then, the survivors began their somber trek home. It was reported that all along the way groups of people gathered in grim silence to watch the bowed passersby in their mute sorrow, and to glimpse the coffins in the wagons. At Natchez, deep in the Archer neighborhood, and where Martin Archer once operated a grocery store, the procession stopped. People from the scattered rural community came out to have the coffins opened, so that they might view their friends now dead. The next day, the three bodies were taken to the edge of West Baden and buried in the Wolfington Cemetery.

It was all over for Thomas, Martin, and John Archer; and even for young Mart Archer, and Samuel A. Bunch. It was not over for Sam Archer, the last member of stature of the Archer Gang who, according to Lynch's testimony, was equally guilty with the others of Bunch's death.

The news of what the vigilantes had done the night of March 9 soon brought to Shoals newspaper reporters from Indianapolis, Vincennes, Cincinnati, Louisville, St. Louis and other distant points. Trains brought them daily, until the grisly story of the retributive execution of the Archer men had been told in almost every city and town. Whole front pages of newspapers were given to the illegal hangings, Lynch's testimony describing the murder of Bunch, and the approaching trial of the last member of the Archer Gang.

On March 24, Samuel Archer and Lynch were brought up by train from Jeffersonville to Shoals by Sheriff Padgett and several armed deputies. Having learned of the transfer of the two prisoners, crowds of people gathered at every station along the way, hoping to catch sight of the two men who would be legally tried for Bunch's murder. Tensions were such when they changed trains at Seymour that the lawmen were reinforced by forty state militiamen. When they at last arrived in Shoals, a huge crowd had collected at the railroad station. Fearing the worst, the militiamen disembarked from the train and formed an armed square. After the manacled Sam Archer and John Lynch were placed in the center of this, the entire contingent marched off through Shoals, across the bridge over White River, and to the jail at West Shoals. At the jail, Samuel Archer, ironically, was locked in the cellblock from which Thomas, Martin, and John Archer had been taken by force by the vigilantes the night of March 9. Lynch was locked in a cell on the jail's upper floor.

At two o'clock in the afternoon of July 23, Judge David J. Hefron called the Martin County Circuit Court into session. Pauper attorneys Eph Moser and H. Q. Houghton, who had been assigned by Hefron to

Sam Archer, announced they were ready for trial. The state's case against Sam Archer and John Lynch was under the direction of prosecutor Hiram McCormick, and "judges" Farrell Gardiner and C. S. Dobbins, his associates. History offers no reason why the two assistant prosecution attorneys were addressed as judge, but it may be presumed that they had once occupied the bench, and use of the title at this time may have been a ploy to place due process in an auspicious light.

When the courtroom clock had ticked away three hours, eight jurors and two alternates were impaneled. They were James P. Walker, George W. Swayzee, William Summerville, Thomas Craig, Samuel Roberts, John B. Chastain, Martin Stout, Edward Coffee, Charles Denny, and John Harp. Hefron then adjourned until the next morning.

Among those witnesses who took the stand in the next few days were the woman who lived with Bunch, a lesser member of the Archer Gang named David Crane, and John Lynch, who had turned state's witness to save himself. The woman testified that she and Bunch were not husband and wife, and that he had left Tennessee after murdering a man there. She revealed that one week after Bunch disappeared, Martin and Sam Archer had come to her house requesting certain writings in her possession concerning Bunch and Sam Marley. She testified that she knew Bunch had met with foul play. When she attempted to learn the whereabouts of his body, because she wanted to give it a decent burial, she said she was warned by Martin and Sam Archer that they could dispose of her as easily as they had Bunch. When Bunch's remains were found, it was she, the woman told the court, who identified the buttons from Bunch's clothing.

Crane's testimony differed little from the woman's, and Lynch's followed the course of his earlier confessions. Less than four days after the start of the trial, early Saturday, July 27, the batteries of attorneys presented final arguments, and the case against Sam Archer, and that against John Lynch, went to the eight men in the jury box. After one hour and thirty minutes of deliberation, they returned with a guilty verdict against Sam Archer, and set his punishment as death. Hefron then announced the manner in which the people requested that Sam Archer die. "Hanged by the neck until dead." He set the time of execution thirteen days later, August 9, 1886. The condemned man was then asked by Hefron if he had anything to say. Sam Archer reportedly replied, "Not at this time."

Hefron was later to overrule a motion for a new trial, and the judge also ruled against a motion for an arrest of sentence. Pleas on behalf of Sam Archer were submitted to the court. Some reached the governor's office, one of which purportedly was made by a monsignor at a Catholic church in Indianapolis. It was said that he was moved by the futile attempts of a Shoals priest, a Father Fitzpatrick, to influence the governor toward clemency. Although Sam Archer was not a Catholic, Fitzpatrick, the record shows, was, for reasons unknown, his spiritual adviser.

When the day of the execution dawned, some six thousand people had gathered in Shoals, drawn there by a morbid desire to watch another human die at the end of a rope. Like religious pilgrims in an impassioned rush to the scene of a miracle, they had come to the Martin County seat on foot, on horseback, in buggies and wagons. They had come by train, in special coaches, filled to overflowing, which the railroad company had conveniently added to its regular trains. They filled the hotels and rooming houses and saloons and restaurants to the bursting point; a roisterous rabble of humans, spending money at a rate never before seen in the town.

Anticipating such a turn of events, the court ordered the gallows on which Sam Archer was to die to be enclosed by a high, board stockade. But the platform, which was twelve feet by sixteen feet, and seventeen feet high, was clearly visible and would offer, without obstruction, the grim spectacle the horde had come to see.

Twelve men were appointed by the court to legally witness Sam Archer's execution from within the high board fence. They were Joseph Ackerman, Peter M. Walker, John T. Huebner, Martin Stout, James P. Walker, Moses Williams, Martin Verry, George Swayzee, John Sherfick, John Arnold, Russell Baker, and John Leitch.

Three Shoals physicians, whose names in old news accounts appear only as Shirley, Plummer and Walls, and Dr. N. W. Beard of Vincennes, and Martin County Coroner Charles Mohr, and reporters from newspapers from all over the midwest, were also present inside the enclosure.

Clinging monkey-like to every available limb and branch, spectators filled the trees outside the fenced-in gallows. Others crowded every crack and knothole in the board fence so that they might capture live every detail of Sam Archer's last seconds of life and his first moments of death. One newspaper account described the scene as ". . . circus-like, attributable to a sickened mob." Another newspaper report noted that ". . . Women, old and young, with children and babies, pushed and shoved in the crowd" around the fence so that they might better see, and that . . . their children might also see." Another newspaper account reported that Shoals " . . . was gripped in a carnival air and a display of utter heartlessness . . . " While the crowd milled and pushed and shoved, the sheriff and several deputies moved into the heaving mass of humanity around the gallows fence to make room for VIPs who held passes for the macabre exhibition.

Meanwhile, Sam Archer, who was waiting to be hanged by the neck until dead, was allowed visitors for the last time. Relatives and friends came to bid him farewell. He was also allowed some time with Father Fitzpatrick, and a Father Slavan. Finally, then, with Sheriff Padgett in the lead, and several deputies around him, Sam Archer, with the two priests following, was ushered toward the scaffold.

When the mob saw the condemned man, there rose from six thousand throats a thunderous, merciless cheer. As suddenly as it had rent the air, the sound abated, and the mass of people watched quietly as the convicted man was led up the gallows steps. A black hood was placed over his head, the noose of the hangman's rope was fitted to his neck, and the trap was sprung. Every move had been timed without interruption so that at thirteen minutes after one o'clock Sam Archer plunged into eternity.

At that very moment, the watching crowd surged maniacally against the stockade " . . . like a mass of madmen . . .," one newspaper reported. In the maelstrom, gates were torn open and boards were ripped off the enclosure, " . . . and the crowd, including women and children, seemingly insane," the report continued, "jammed the stockade and gaped at the form kicking in mid-air, as though fascinated by the horrible sight . . . "

At two o'clock the esteemed physicians examined the corpse of Sam Archer and agreed that he was dead, and his body was cut down and carried away from the crowd into the courthouse. This was accomplished with the only touch of dignity afforded the legal execution – it was carried in a coffin that had been brought earlier for that purpose. The body was released to the mother of the dead man. Later, after some argument by the members of a church who did not want "Sam Archer" buried in their cemetery, it was interred in the Ames Cemetery.

Lynch, in payment for his services to the people, was sentenced to prison for three years. Another member of the Archer Gang, Charles Parker, twenty-six, pleaded guilty to a horse stealing charge and Hefron sentenced him to seven years. Vigilantes seized gang member Kinder Smith, a nephew of old Martin Archer, and "strung" him up to a tree three times, then gave him forty lashes and twenty-four hours to get out of Martin County.

Still other members of the gang were sent to prison on lesser charges, and those who could not be proven guilty of crimes soon learned they were no longer wanted in Lost River Valley.

JOE BRINEGAR

There were times, when leaving Bloomfield, I returned to my little office room at the newspaper by a route I called "the back way." It's still there. A narrow blacktop that winds eastward from State Road 231 south of Bloomfield. It took me past Furnace, through Mineral City, Koleen and Dresden, then ended at State Road 58, at Owensburg.

On the first few of those trips, I was attracted to an aging country church on the north side of the road, and an adjacent cemetery. In faded letters on a board sign that stretched above the church doorway, the name Ashcraft Chapel became a curiosity to me. On those occasions, I walked among the tombstones in the cemetery to read the legends chiseled into their faces. Except for a blue tent erected over an open grave there one day, the place was deserted, undisturbed, quiet, remote.

Each time I stopped there I'd wondered about the name Ashcraft. That it was a family name was well established in my mind after having seen it on the church building and on some tombstones. But, in all my years of roving, I had never spoken with anyone by that name, nor with anyone who ever indicated a tie to that family. Never, at least, until I spoke with Joe Brinegar at Oolitic one day. Joe informed me that his mother was an Ashcraft; Clyde Jesse Ashcraft having been her maiden name. Since Joe said she had come from Owensburg, I took it for granted that she was part of the Ashcraft Chapel Ashcraft family.

Not that it mattered whether she was or wasn't; it was just a thought that struck me while Joe and I talked in Bob Sharr's Market. He'd been telling me about "Big Joe Brinegar," his father, who worked as a hooker and scabbler during the salad days of Indiana limestone, when Clyde Jessie's name came up. Thinking I might be tempted to wonder, because Clyde — and even Jessie — is more a man's appellation than a woman's, Joe had cautioned me after speaking his mother's first name. There was no need. I had learned early on in interviewing people for my column not to be surprised at names. The name Clyde for a southern Indiana female was no more startling to me than the name Clare, Gladys, or Shirley, for a southern Indiana male.

Joe had spoken his mother's given name while telling me about how his father had to tack a large comforter over a bedroom window to help keep Joe and Clyde warm when Joe was born during the winter of 1917. And Joe went on to say that he was still

130

living in that same house. Wherever I happen on them, people who've lived their lives in a single house, a single community, are a fascination for me. I can never get my fill of hearing them tell me what it was like. How good and satisfying it was.

"It's home," Joe answered my query. "It's a place to put your feet. If it wasn't my birthplace and home-place, I'd have put it up for sale long ago and left. But there are too many memories there."

He related some. One was of a switching from Clyde. "I hit the floor crying," he recalled, "and she said, 'You might just as well lay there and take it.' Which I did. But I still cried and kicked. But that switching never hurt me," he vowed. "It did me some good."

Had it not been for being drafted at the beginning of World War II, Joe might never have spent a day away from his birthplace. Those were the days when Greyhound buses stopped daily at crossroads all over the nation to pick up young men and delivered them to induction centers. When Joe boarded the bus that stopped for him, it was the first time he had ever left his Oolitic. One of the luckier of the tens of thousands of servicemen and women who would never return from that war, Joe came back to Oolitic. He had served fifty-four months in the Army and fought in France, Belgium, Holland and Germany with the 638th Tank Destroyer Battalion. He was awarded, among other decorations, the Purple Heart.

Three years after Joe got home, Big Joe fell and struck his head and died. Joe put his own life's desires aside to remain with his widowed mother. After having been an invalid for many years, during which time Joe cared for her, she passed away in 1968 at the age of ninety.

"I enjoyed it," he said of the years he spent with Clyde Jessie. "We had our arguments, our naggings.

But I enjoyed it. I enjoyed her in sickness and in health. It wasn't easy by no means. But Mom had told me more than once, 'Don't ever put me in a nursing home.' I didn't. I was able to handle things with the help of a lady who came to the house in the daytime. See, I had to work during the day."

At this time, almost twenty years had passed since Clyde Jessie died. Almost twice that much time had passed since Big Joe died. You'd think a person would forget. In Joe's case it hadn't worked out that way.

"Time goes by, the years go by, but you know, you still miss them," he said. "The memories are still there. I could walk away from them, I guess. I could live elsewhere. I did during the war for more than four years. But I won't. This is a kind of pretty nice, friendly town, and it's not bad to live in the same town all of your life. You see a lot of people leave, and a lot of them die. And it gets lonesome when you've lost your loved ones. But this is not bad. I have a place to sleep. I come up to town every day and visit places, and I see my friends every day."

THE WAKE

Roy Legge should've had his name in the newspaper several times; he was that interesting a person. His name did appear on our front page once. It was a couple or three elections past; the time he was beaten out of Bean Blossom Township's first voter honors by Vern Glidden. Roy had to walk more than two miles to the polls that morning, and Vern rode in a car; even passed Roy while he was walking.

Vern was determined to do it. He didn't care that he was less than half Roy's age. He didn't care that it was a matter of pride to the older man to walk more than two miles to vote in every election. It was obvious that Roy was being very American, and he was doing it the hard way, the way folks used to in the old days.

Roy had done more than walk a couple or more miles to the polls every election day. He was a college graduate, for one thing; held a degree in engineering. In his time, he taught at Bunker Hill and other schools in Monroe County. He also rode a bicycle more miles, perhaps, than any person most people can think of. He toured the United States on a bicycle. He was injured at least three times in auto-bike accidents, which is a lot of times and still live to tell it.

During World War I he served with the American Expeditionary Forces in France; he collected stamps, wired railroad signals, worked in a post office, and, when rural electrification became a reality, he set about wiring almost every house in Bean Blossom Township, and in Gosport across the river.

It was toward the end of March, in 1976. We were seated on and around the Liar's Bench in Bob Summitt's Grocery Store in Stinesville: Frank Ellett, Ralph Parrish, and Beverly Summitt, who was minding the store while her husband was out of town. We had buried Roy earlier that day, and we were finding it difficult to let go of his memory.

Ralph remembered when Roy wired his house. "His charge was twenty dollars," Ralph said. "But when I went to pay him he said, 'You don't owe me that much. I worked three days and your wife gave me dinner three days, so I marked off a quarter a day. All you owe me is nineteen twenty-five.' "

That was many years ago, but it's only one more example of the kind of guy Roy was all his life. Reporters could have written many good stories about him. We didn't. When he died, we had the chance to say something good about him, and what did we do? We printed his name wrong in the paper. Instead of Roy Legge in the headline of his obituary, we printed *Wayne* Legge.

There wasn't a Wayne Legge in the whole county. There was no damn reason for us to do what we did. But, we did it. I later talked with Roy's sister, Lucille Van Buskirk, and she confirmed the error. I apologized, but the damage was done. Of course, we ran a correction, but people who read mistakes in newspapers rarely see the corrections. You can bet on that.

We still do that sort of thing. A man lives a good life, adheres to the Golden Rule, votes in every election, and what does he get? His name spelled wrong in his obituary. Some crooked politician kicks the bucket and we don't allow a single typo to appear in all the lies and false claims printed about him. I'm sure our reward awaits us – someplace.

These are the things we talked about, there in the store, after Roy's funeral. You might say it was a wake, of sorts, for Roy. A wake around the Liar's Bench.

Frank told us that Roy once bought eighty dozen canning lids and sent them to friends in the South who were too poor to buy them. They had the jars, but no lids. One of Roy's more recent experiences was a bus trip that took him into thirty states, Frank said.

While we were thus engrossed, Ella Arnett and Ilene Baker came into the store. Ellie – that's what Ella went by in Stinesville – was a respected and respectable lady. She went to church at least three times a week, and, if there was a revival within reaching distance, she'd go to that too.

Ellie avowed that the Lord had been good to her, and that His grace had been sufficient, and that sometimes she'd even go to church four times a week. She talked about Esther Kell, another of Roy's sisters, who was a childhood friend. Frank interrupted to say that Ilene was the best donut maker in Stinesville, and Ilene said, "For the ones that begs me like he does, I guess I am." Then Frank said something about Ellie riding a motorcycle, and Ilene's donuts were forgotten.

"It was beautiful weather," Ellie began recounting the experience after scolding Frank for bringing it up. "The raspberries were ripe and I'd taken a bucket along with me. And here comes this girl on a motorcycle, and she said, 'You want a lift?' And I said, 'Why of course.' And I got on."

Ellie was eighty-two, with not enough spring in her bones to be riding on a tricycle, let alone a motorcycle. But people knew better than to try to tell her that. Anyway, they said that when she got on that motorcycle she broke the law – she wasn't wearing a helmet. She also broke something else that day – when they saw her riding into town on the back end of a motorcycle like that, the kids in Stinesville fell apart.

" 'Here comes Ellie on a MOTORCYCLE!' They all hooted and hollered," Ellie remembered. "I was wearing a skirt, and I know it showed my legs when I was riding that thing, and I'm not one to show my legs."

"That's not all," Frank interrupted from the overstuffed chair that flanked the Liar's Bench. He held closed fists up to his ears with the thumbs extended outward. "Her hair was sticking out both ways."

"My children didn't hardly appreciate it," Ellie continued as though she hadn't heard Frank. "But I love to ride on a motorcycle. My daughter that lives here said she believed I was losing my mind."

During the telling of the motorcycle ride, Joe Dillman, who drove a fuel truck for Farm Bureau Co-op, came in, as did Jim Arnett, Don Arthur, and Bud Halstead, Beverly's brother. Mary Anderson came in a little later. Little Kenny Barnes came in, too, and Frank dug down in a pocket and gave him a stick of Spearmint gum.

When little Amy Summitt came in, Beverly's niece, Frank gave her some nickels. She told Frank that she would put them in the First National Bank in Bloomington. She added, for his information, that she was also going to put in the bank three quarters the tooth fairy had left her under her pillow the previous night. The tooth fairy, she smiled, had left them in payment for a new wide gap quite obvious in the front of her upper teeth.

Frank was probably as old as Ellie, or older. For a few years he kept promising to come out to visit me at my place. But he just couldn't seem to pull himself out of the overstuffed chair Bob had put in the store. Bob tried to make loungers comfortable and secure. He even took the time to nail some risers on the front legs of the Liar's Bench. They tilted the front up enough so that the knee-slappers, in their exuberance at the whoppers told there, wouldn't slide off and maybe hurt themselves.

Frank let a cat out of the bag. Ellie and one of her sisters once found their father's peach brandy in the garden while they were weeding. They got smashed. Ellie wanted me to promise to tell none of this "Or I'll get churched," she said. "Excommunicated," she explained. "I go to the Nazarene Church, but I'm a Seventh Day Adventist," she said. She threatened Frank. "Frank, I'll kick you in the shin if you don't hush." But she was smiling, and Frank just went on giving more of her secrets away.

Roy came back into the conversation, and I remembered that early election morning when he came in second to Vern at the polls. The polling place was in the elementary school and I was there with my camera. Some people were lined up in the school hallway while they waited for six o'clock and the voting to start. They kidded Roy about losing out to Vern. Roy kidded right back. But I know he was hurt, and perhaps somewhat humbled, even if he was being a good sport about it. It's enough for older people to be old without having to be old and humiliated, too. Roy was never first to vote after that. Never talked about being first anymore. Acted like he didn't care.

I tried to picture him, tall, bespectacled, with that gray-striped railroad cap he always wore just so on his head, and sitting there in the store with us, and

137

laughing, and joking around. But he was not there. He was dead. We had buried him earlier that day.

I felt a kind of fullness deep inside myself. Love, I figured; an old love for Stinesville, for some of its people, and Roy among them, making itself known again. I wished again that we had written more about him while he was alive. I especially ached that we had used someone else's name instead of his in the headline on his obituary.

Ralph Scott

CLEAR SPRING

During a basketball game that saw the Clear Spring Greyhounds on their way to a shellacking by the Freetown Spartans, coach Ralph Scott glared across the floor to where Spartan coach Edgar Sprague was sitting. Then, turning to an assistant, Scott growled in Hoosier idiom, "I had a chance to get rid of that guy one time, but I let my skimmer leak, and I saved him."

Scott later recounted the incident. He said that he had gone soft one day years earlier while he and

Sprague, as young sprouts and lifelong friends, were sporting around in Scott's roadster. As they neared Jonesville, Scott lost control of the car and it overturned, throwing Scott clear and pinning Sprague underneath the wreck. Scott could never explain how it was possible, and two persons tried unsuccessfully to equal his feat afterward, but he lifted and held the roadster off his injured friend until Sprague could crawl to safety.

"That was before we began coaching," Scott told me many years later in Brownstown, where he was a successful businessman. "We were good friends then and we were good friends when we coached. But I always was a bad loser. I would rather a guy take a club and beat my ears off as to lose a basketball game."

The feeling was never stronger than it was the year Clear Spring was suspended by the IHSAA. "We were supposed to have imported a boy from Bedford to play ball for us," said Scott recalling the alleged grounds for the boot. The incident goes back to the 1930s, and it is still remembered by Clear Spring alums. The father of a Bedford basketball player purportedly was given a job as school custodian, plus a rent-free house for him and his family, so that the young man could play for Clear Spring.

Was Clear Spring guilty?

"I don't know," Scott answered through a larger than life smile. "The IHSAA said we were. I never said we did anything like that. That boy just happened to be a good ballplayer, and his dad just happened to go to work for the school, and he just happened to move his family to Clear Spring."

The youth was, in fact, an excellent ballplayer, and Clear Spring that year had fielded one of its better teams. But, because of the suspension, the high school team played only a few independent games,

140

and Greyhound fans were deprived of their usual winter entertainment. A few years later, the world was at war, and although Scott and Clear Spring alums never forgot or forgave the suspension – and what brought it about – the young man involved was forgotten. At the outset of the war, he joined the Army Air Corps, and, as Captain Hamel Goodin, led the first B-17 bomber raid on Berlin. Goodin further distinguished himself for the duration of World War II and for many years afterward. At the time of his retirement from the U.S. Air Force, he had attained the rank of colonel.

Alums did not forget Scott. He had helped to give the Jackson County "country" school an identity. As a student there, he played forward with a degree of distinction for coaches Henry McHargue and Roy C. Bullington. He played alongside such country greats as Orville Brown, Kenneth Weininger, Clyde Sutton and Raymond Hinderlider. After studying at Indiana Central at Indianapolis, and Central Normal at Danville, Scott taught a year each at schools in Liberty, Norman and Elkinsville. He then was called to teach at his alma mater.

Floyd Starke was basketball coach at Clear Spring then. Besides teaching farm shop and phys-ed to seventh and eighth graders, Scott was given the second team to coach. As a consolidated school, Clear Spring's enrollment in grades one through twelve was usually more than five hundred, and there were plenty of kids to go around. Herbert Fish, Wayne Fish, Bill Louden, Lawrence Christie and James Brooking made up the second team. Scott wasn't with them for long, although he'd see them again; Starke moved to Medora in Scott's first year at Clear Spring, and Scott was elevated to coach of the varsity team. Hollis Black, Ross Beavers, Ralph Mitchener, Earl

141

Coleman, Charlie Morrison and Audie Ratliff were its members. They were to be his best team in the several years he coached at the school.

"We won fourteen in a row that year," Scott recalled, his face flushing with the memory. "That was the year the newspaper nicknamed us the Clear Spring Giants; because we were good, and because the team's average height was six feet. That was tall in those days."

There wasn't much to the town of Clear Spring itself in those days; an auto repair garage and a couple stores. But kids – the school had plenty. They came from around the countryside, including Houston, after the school there closed its doors, and several came from various branches of a large family surnamed "Fish."

"There was a time Clear Spring could have started five Fishes," Scott remembered. "And the *Indianapolis Star* said that Clear Spring that year was the 'Fishiest' town in the state."

They are not to be confused with the Fisher brothers who surfaced in Clear Spring basketball before Scott's coaching days there. They were Walter, who went on to coach at Muncie Central, George, who coached at Warsaw, and Scott Fisher who coached at Seymour and then went on to Burris at Muncie.

Scott left coaching early in life and went into private business, first in Clear Spring and then in Brownstown. He kept abreast of basketball via the sports pages and TV. His name cropped up every so often in local basketball lore and in the fifty-year looking back columns of the newspaper.

"The last time my name was in the paper while I was still active in basketball," he confided to me during our visit, "was about my officiating, which I did for a while after I quit coaching. In a game between Vallonia and Medora I called forty-four fouls. The newspaper called me 'The Whistle-Tooter'."

Some months after Clear Spring closed and its kids transferred to Brownstown, I spoke with a few of them. It was their consensus, as spoken by Jeff Fisher, that they preferred going to Clear Spring "Because the teachers were better, and you stayed in one room all day, and you made better grades in that school," and they didn't have to ride a bus to get to it.

It is doubtful that anyone will ever again attend classes in the Clear Spring schools. Mable Brown who once taught there felt the full disappointment of that truth when she visited there from Franklin, where she was teaching school. So did former teachers Joe Bevers, who had retired from a long principalship in Seymour elementary schools; Ray Smith, who taught at Brownstown; Shirley Keper, from Franklin; Myron Curry, who taught at Seymour and had also attended Clear Spring, and taught there; and Ray Aynes, who was born and reared in Clear Spring, and graduated from high school there and had retired from teaching in Brownstown. As a group they had visited Clear Spring to take another look at the high school, the oldest of Clear Spring's three abandoned school buildings. Pearl Howe, who taught there and made her home in Clear Spring, saw those empty buildings every day.

The date chiseled into a limestone inlay high up on the former high school's brick facade stands out as "A.D. 1923." The message recounts nothing of the souls that learned behind the brick walls, nor does it indicate their number. Fourteen-year-old Jeff was one of them. He had attended kindergarten there, as did Greg Patton, who was the same age, and Steve Charles, who was fifteen. They were among the last pupils to sit in the old school's six upper classrooms, and to run through its small gym.

Clear Spring school days may have been better days for school kids. Steve liked them because school

143

was nearer home, and Mike Hoaks, who was twenty-one at the time of my visit, who attended school there for ten years, said, "You could do more at Clear Spring, and you could make the team. When we had to go to Brownstown there were more people, so many people you couldn't make the team."

Frank Cummings made the team at Clear Spring, and he went on to play for Purdue, and then returned to Clear Spring to teach. Larry Garloch also made the team and played through his sophomore year there, before he went on to Brownstown, and later to star at Miami of Ohio; and fellows like Dean Zike, then teaching in Mt. Vernon and Dwight Fisher. There was a time Clear Spring's roar was heard around Hoosierland, when its school could be counted on to be a tough contender for the state's top high school basketball honors. If A.D. 1923 could speak, and recount the years since then, the pupils, the teachers, the deeds, the basketball games! What a story compared to the heartbreak of broken and shattered windows I saw there.

"I die a little bit every time I go in there," said Daniel Boone (Dan) Horton Jr. He spent nineteen years in the old brick. Reared in the Clear Spring neighborhood, he graduated in 1956. After his graduation from Indiana University, in Bloomington, Horton returned to Clear Spring to teach for two years, and then spent another five years there as its principal. After taking a master's degree in secondary education at IU, and later earning a doctorate in education there, he moved on to Indiana State University in Terre Haute. But Horton was unable to escape the slow death of the school of his childhood and early teaching years. He owned the building, and the ten acres on which it was situated. He also owned the elementary school building across the road from it, and a portable classroom next to that.

"The elementary school building site was a part of our farm," Horton said. The additional ten acres extended the Horton farm to approximately five hundred and sixty acres. A new roof had been put on the portable classroom building. The high school gym, which opened off the corridor of the main floor, also was covered with a new roof. "Getting them under new roof," was Horton's main objective while he pondered a future for the three buildings. The gym, he said, may provide temporary storage for hay. He and his wife, Helen Battram Horton, who taught at Bedford High School, purchased the township land and school buildings a year before my visit. Although they were undecided about the future of the old buildings, they had been selling the schools' old desks.

When the high school yearbook "Crusader" made its appearance in Clear Spring in 1936, it consisted of typewritten pages reproduced on a duplicator or mimeo, and snapshots pasted in the cord-bound album. It was the work of that year's class: Max Hanners, Pat Murphy, Carl Fish, Joe Goen, Luther Kirby, Katherine Kindred, Dorothy Christie, Maxine Styers, Velma Norman, Bernard Hurley, Gaylous Easton, Carl Fox and Earl Davidson.

At least one copy was to survive forty-two years, and was in the hands of one of those graduates, a white-haired Maxine Styers Goen. When I called on Mrs. Goen, she and a sister-in-law, Dillie May Brooks, had been to a funeral and were reminiscing over coffee, as people will do after attending such a service. Dillie May, who lived in Ashland City, Tennessee, graduated from Clear Spring the year before Mrs. Goen. The deceased, whose funeral brought the two women together, was Dillie May's eldest sister, Jeannette Barrett, who was living in Boswell, near Lafayette, at the time of her death. Another Clear

Spring alum, Mrs. Barrett, later taught at Dodd School near there.

Mrs. Goen met and married her late husband, Tommy, at Clear Spring. Folks traveling any distance often rode school buses back then. One day when Tommy was on his way to Johnny and Sally McCullough's to cut wood, he stopped the bus Maxine was riding to school and climbed aboard carrying his axe. Their eyes met and less than a couple of years later they were married. Tommy, and his sister, Stella Reinbold, of Brownstown, set a record for attendance at Clear Spring that was never broken. From the first grade through twelfth, they didn't miss a single day. Mrs. Goen's son, Dennis, was a member of the Bloomington Fire Department. Another son, Danny Goen, was a member of the Franklin Fire Department. Her daughter, Shirley Beasley, and Shirley's husband, Allen, operated a chicken farm near Mrs. Goen's home. Mrs. Goen recalled an old joke that poked fun at Clear Spring because of its size. A mythical intersection at the tiny community's center – the joke goes – was made up of Poke and Plum streets. A motorist, it continues, had little chance of seeing that intersection, or surrounding Clear Spring, because "By the time you poke your head out of the window, Clear Spring is plumb gone."

In Clear Spring, and among its sons and daughters, wherever they may be, the joke about Poke and Plum streets is a knee-slapper. It speaks of something the rest of us can never understand. So, we are cautioned, don't poke around trying to plumb its depths.

Pictured, from left, Shirley Jackson, her son, infant Dale Jackson, and store clerk Rita Carr.

LEHMAN'S STORE

During the long months Owensburg brothers Bob and Pete Lehman were trying to sell their general store and embark on a well-earned retirement, I was secretly sticking sharp little pins into the doll of their dream. Yet, I did write a column about their wish to sell, and, after the sale was consummated, I found myself hoping that in some small way it had helped them. But I really didn't want them to quit; I loved the old store the way it was, complete with Bob and Pete somewhere in its depths.

I was not alone in my regret at the loss. No one in the whole of that small Greene County community could remember shopping there when a Lehman didn't own the place and wasn't there to greet and serve

147

them. The first time I visited there – a wandering reporter in search of a column subject – Bob and Pete were present as working owners. The date escapes me now, but I do remember that we hit it off from the start. And when I announced the reason for that first visit, they volunteered the interesting history of Lehman's.

The brothers had shared ownership of the store ever since 1949 when their father, Evert Lehman, decided it would be more profitable to sell the store to his sons rather than remain as a partner. And since Bob and Pete were the last Lehmans to do business in Owensburg, their departure marked the end of an era that began more than one hundred years earlier.

It was in 1867 that Pennsylvania Dutch-born Peter C. Lehman opened his cabinet and coffin shop there. By virtue of being the coffin maker, Peter was also the community undertaker. His parents had settled north of Bloomfield, but on Peter's return from service in the Civil War he was lured to Owensburg by pretty Martha Stine who lived there. Twelve children were born to their subsequent marriage, one of whom was Evert. And it was he who would join his father and continue the Lehman name in the cabinet shop and undertaking business there.

Another town enterprise of that period was W. S. (Sammy) Sentney's Grocery Store which was founded on a site later occupied by a structure that became popularly known as "Mrs. Osborne's house." Sammy and his wife, Clementine, had a daughter named Clara, and she and Evert became friends, fell in love, and married in 1892. The son of the coffin maker and undertaker then went to work for his wife's father in the grocery store.

A year later Sentney's was leveled by fire. According to a Bloomfield newspaper, Sammy's investment in the store and stock before the destructive blaze was $4,800 and he received a $6,000 settlement from an insurance company. However, he decided against rebuilding and opened a store in a structure already standing in the town. Apparently undamaged by fire, Sammy's safe was removed from the gutted building to the new location. It later became a popular conversation piece since it not only had escaped destruction by fire, it also had been dynamited open by thieves in 1887 and the combination lock was never repaired. It was a kind of joke, too, that should a holdup occur the robber should be advised not to shoot, the safe was unlocked, and that he should help himself.

After the fire Sammy also opened a store on the east side of the public square in downtown Bloomington. The Owensburg store came into the Lehman family in 1922, when Evert bought it from his father-in-law. Because he had continued with his father's business of burying the dead, Evert, after that, began wearing two hats, one as the town's storekeeper and the other as its undertaker.

Two of his and Clara's eleven children would follow in his footsteps, Bob and Pete. And, in 1948, a generous Evert took them in as partners. But at the completion of that calendar year, after father and sons determined they each had earned only $900 for the twelve-month period, Evert had an announcement to make. He had traced the lack of profits to the over extension of credit to customers, and a poor collection effort by his novice partners.

"If this is the way you guys are going to run a store," he delivered a memorable ultimatum, "then I want out."

By this time Bob and Pete were married and for a time the financial situation of the new owners was serious. Bob, who went to work in the store for his father as a teenager and was paid ten dollars a week, once gave an insight to their plight.

"During that time we were struggling, and I often thought I would have been better off to have continued working for my father for ten dollars a week," he said.

While still a youth, Bob had assisted his father in the undertaking business and had accompanied him to private homes to help embalm the dead. After a 1938 state law put an end to that practice, Evert opened a licensed preparation room in the store's warehouse. Later a modern funeral parlor was established in Bob's home, across the street from the general store.

Bob carried on the Lehman undertaking tradition until 1964 when the store's increasing success began demanding all the time both brothers could give it. Bob had fond memories of his days as a mortician. Proud of the years he had given to the profession, he once said that there is nothing a person can do that will be more appreciated by people than being an undertaker.

"We always had some interested spectators when we prepared a corpse in a home," he recalled his early days in the business. "Folks stayed up with their dead at least two nights, and everybody liked to have a Sunday funeral. You see, you'd have a bigger crowd on Sunday, and if somebody died as early in the week as Wednesday, it was sure he would have a Sunday funeral."

Bob brought out an old ledger in which a December 26, 1868 entry by grandfather Peter Lehman revealed the price of a coffin to be twenty-two dollars, and the price of a picket fence around a grave was fifteen dollars. It was also noted in the ledger that Greene County had at that time paid one dollar and fifty-cents a casket foot for coffins for paupers. A six-foot coffin at that rate came to nine dollars. At the time Bob showed me the old ledger, an oak casket made by Grandfather Lehman was on display at Ferguson Lee Funeral Home in Bedford, and a baby-size casket was on display at Welch and Cornett Funeral Home in Linton. As late as 1963, the average cost per funeral in Owensburg was three hundred dollars, Bob said.

Some years after Bob had terminated the under-taking business, he and his wife, Delpha, and their young son, Van, were cleaning out a storage building near the store. While moving things around, Bob and Delpha discovered a vintage casket that went back to his father's early days as a mortician. Delpha, a registered nurse and helpmate to Bob when the mortuary was in their home, was not repelled by the things associated with death. On seeing the old casket, she giggled and said to her husband, "I'll bet I can fit into that," and before Bob could object she climbed into the coffin and stretched out in mock repose.

"Close the lid," she had a sudden thought. "And call Van."

When Van responded to his father's summons, Bob slowly raised the coffin lid. Shocked at the sight of what he thought was a dead person, Van gasped and shrank backward. Then he recognized his mother. "Boy, Dad!" he said with a huge sigh of relief, "for a minute I thought Grandpaw had forgot to bury somebody."

Very little happened in and around Owensburg that wasn't discussed at Lehman's. While some of it may not have been printable, it was, as almost anything is in a family, discussable. Lehman's indeed was like family, and, more than anything about the sale of the store, I am convinced it was the break-up of the family aspect of the place that pained me. It was unlike any other store I'd ever been in. In the words of Owensburg resident and store customer Gene Roberts, "Going to Lehman's was like going to a circus."

At times it was indeed. There were a number of old hickory chairs held together with binder twine that hosted yarn spinners the likes of Hester Jackson, Bob Hudson, Ora (Poke) Harp, his brother, Dennis (Snoog) Harp, Huckleberry Hannon, Wayne Reed, Sam Thomasson and Grandpaw Gardner.

Bob once said that if you could turn yourself into a little mouse and hide near those chairs and listen, you could learn a lot. I was unable to turn myself into a little mouse, but I stood there numerous times, and I did glean some knowledge. For instance, did you know that a raindrop falling on Ilene Roberts' house could conceivably separate with half ending up in the East Fork of White River and the other half running down the West Fork, and becoming one again at the confluence of the two streams.

Ilene's house is on a high hogback, its roof canted on one side to the east and on the other side to the west. Rainwater cascading off the east side ran into Indian Creek while rainwater spilling off the west side ran into Plummer's Creek. The sages who had worked out this phenomenon held that a single raindrop could separate at the point of the roof, and that the two parts could be rejoined somewhere north of Petersburg. Long before that reunion, the eastbound half of the raindrop, they noted, would have had to traverse Indian Creek to Trinity Springs, a distance of some forty miles, before entering the east fork of the river. Its westbound counterpart in Plummer's Creek would enter the west fork near Bloomfield, only a few miles away.

I was in Lehman's one day when two proud parents brought their infant child to be weighed on the counter scale. It was a common occurrence; parents weighed their new babies there. The Dwight Craig family of eight children were weighed on that scale. And the Zebedee Rush family of five were weighed there, also the Ralph Rainey's nine children, the Everett O'Bannon's five, Paul and Rose Moffit's five, Denny Fields' three, and all his grandchildren and great grandchildren. There was the Jackson family, too, Daniel, Lois, Lonnie and Ruth Ann, in that order. Soon after they were born, their parents, Carl and Pansy, hiked to Lehman's and weighed them in. They also weighed their babies at home. "But," Pansy said, "it was on one of those dangling scales; you know, they held the ring on their finger and it jiggled up and down. That kind was never accurate."

"I couldn't begin to count the number of babies that have been weighed on this old scale," Bob once observed. "We've had this one since 1930. Bringing babies in to get them weighed was a big thing here at one time. People still bring their babies in to weigh them."

To the best of his recollection, no serious mishap ever occurred during the weigh-ins. No infant ever rolled off the scale to crash to the floor, and, on balance, none had any other kind of accident on the scale, he said.

I had developed such a filial attachment for Lehman's that I traveled to and from some other communities via that place. A trip to Loogootee, Shoals, Koleen, Mineral, Furnace, Bloomfield, Switz City and Linton all provided the excuse I needed to stop at the store on the way or on the way back. It was a great place to visit at lunch time. A sandwich from the meat case was always available with the "fixin's," along with a seat in one of the rickety hickory chairs. And there was always a cold drink available to go with it.

I was able to make many new acquaintances there and to learn from each stop who in the town and surrounding area was sick, who had a new baby, who had died, and so many other interesting community happenings. For the recently bereaved, there was placed on the counter a small rectangular box with a slot in the lid in which money for floral condolences was inserted. There was always an accompanying writing tablet in which donors signed their names.

For years, Bob and Pete's sister, Mary Louise Buher, worked there with them, but by the time I found the place, she had fallen ill and had to retire. There were eleven Lehman children. Evert kept a photograph of his large family, with him standing in the foreground, hanging from a wall in the store. An unknowing salesman seeing it one day observed, "Why, Mr. Lehman, I didn't know that you taught school."

The general store was one of a kind, dealing in stoves, mowers, hardware, groceries, meats, dry goods – bolts of colorful cloth on shelves (like in the old days) – clothing, shoes, and almost anything else one might think of. The store was the only local shopping place for Owensburg's five hundred souls. It was also the heart of the small community. Those residents who had no telephone walked to the store to use the one there. The store telephone came in handy for other reasons. One winter day Josie Hayes called the store to say that her toilet had frozen, and she needed help. Lee Bever, the meat cutter, took off his white apron, picked up a torch in the hardware section, and went to Josie's aid. When he returned, he put away the torch, washed his hands, put on the white apron and went back to his job.

I took Bob's word that the population of Owensburg was five hundred. When I asked how he knew, he responded to my obvious doubt by suggesting that I go out and count them. "You may have to go out of town to find them all, but there are five hundred," he said. Then he added, "I've been saying it for thirty years, five hundred."

Few days passed at Lehman's without some visitor announcing that he or she once lived in Owensburg, or that he or she was born there and was taken away at an early age. Myrtle Hudson, of Springville, came "avisiting" one day when I was there, and Bob remembered that as a kid he'd beaten a washtub at her shivaree when she married Homer. Myrtle and Mildred Jean, of Bedford, and Mildred's sister, Anna Wright, of Bloomington, had stopped by after visiting Rock Spring, near Koleen. Myrtle recounted how, when she was a little girl, she and her brother bought a dog there with her three pennies and his two and gave it a bath in the spring. They had the dog for twelve years, and its name was Penny, she said.

Lehman's was a busy place, and helping Bob and Pete at various times were clerks Leona "Babe" Jackson, Rita Carr, Mary Bever, Kay Wilson and Toby Fields. Kathleen, Pete's wife, and Delpha, Bob's wife, also lent a hand.

You could still buy blue jeans for $11.95, the day I tried on a new pair in the small restroom in Lehman's. I wouldn't have been in there except the tag on the jeans showed one size and the Lehman yardstick placed along the inseam gave another, and Pete suggested I try them on for fit.

To say the restroom was small is an understatement. Depending on the gender of the visitor, and his or her need, it was better to either walk straight in or back in, it was so small. There was hardly enough room to turn around, and it was incredible to note that, after all the necessary things had been installed in there, a wastebasket was somehow squeezed into the place.

155

It took some undoing but I managed to take off my shoes and pants. Then holding my pants under one arm I shoved one foot into a leg of the board-stiff new jeans. When I tried the same movement with my other foot, I got it caught in the crotch and lost my balance. I bumped a hip into the wash basin, thumped my head against a wall, and hit my backside on the door-knob. I was trapped, and to stay upright I did some hoppity-hops from the floor to the toilet lid, against the wash basin, and into the wastebasket. Thankfully, there was no window large enough or I might have pitched headlong in my shirttail into the private yard adjacent to the store.

Lehman's has been gone several years now, and one would think I should be able to forget it. There are times when I can. But there are also times when I stick my foot into a pair of jeans that it all comes back to me like I was there only yesterday.

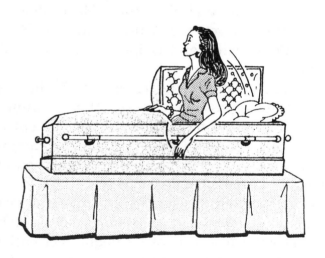

LOWELL DAVIS

Miles of yarns have been spun by newspapermen about how and why they became what they are, and I've heard my share of them. This is yet another one, a story about a young man who was destined to be a school teacher and became, instead, a newspaperman.

At a time during that period when Claude Reynolds owned a barber shop on Main Street, in Mitchell, Indiana State University had graduated a young man named Lowell Davis. Having been born into a family of teachers, he had prepared himself in college to be a shop teacher, and he was looking for such a position.

"At that time, I had received and was considering a contract from a school in Tampa, Florida," Lowell told me during a lunch hour one day in a Mitchell restaurant. "But that was a long way to go in those days. Besides that," he hurried to add with a hint of a smile, "I was in love then, and that was an awful thing to combat."

Lowell began his education in that era when schools were devoid of expensive athletic facilities. Kids got their exercise running trap lines before school hours, doing morning and evening chores at home, and walking to classes.

"The teacher carried an axe in his buggy," Lowell remembered another form of exercise of that time, "and he'd chop a tree and we'd pack the wood to the one room schoolhouse to burn in the stove for heat. That was the only way we could stay warm in school. It was an invaluable experience, and it was an opportunity for kids to learn to share, and to understand and help one another."

Among the schools he attended were two that held special meaning for him. One was situated on the square in Orleans, and it occupied that area usually reserved for a courthouse. It is no longer there. But one of Lowell's memorable school-day treats was Herle's Cafe, on the east side of the square and across the state highway from the school. "I was one of their best customers," he said.

The other school was at Orangeville. After completing the eighth grade there Lowell received his diploma. "Johnny Campbell ran the general store at Orangeville, and a kid who was willing to rise early and run a trap line before school could earn himself fifteen cents. Johnny paid that much for some pelts, and a little more for some others," he said.

Distance being a factor in school attendance, many kids ended their studies after completing the eighth grade. In Lowell's case, since it had already been determined by his parents that he was to become a school teacher, a room was rented for him a couple of miles from Orleans, enabling him to walk to the school on the square.

"I never rode a school bus in my life," he declared with an obvious sense of pride. "But back then we didn't let the government do anything for us. We did what we had to do without help, without asking for help."

College was the great experience of youth. Lowell, who had never been out of the county suddenly found himself boarding a brightly painted, wooden

158

Milwaukee Railroad coach, at Bedford, bound for Terre Haute. When a group of happy college-bound youths boarded the train at Williams, Lowell spotted a pretty girl among them. She was Mabel Barnes, whose parents lived near the Stumphole Bridge. And just like that, he fell for her. By the time he had completed his studies at Indiana State University, he was head over heels in love with her.

It was while he was seriously weighing the advantages of the Tampa contract against his love for Mabel that Lowell walked into Claude Reynolds' barber shop for a haircut. It was a far-out sight in barber shops, even then, but a woman occupied the single chair, and Claude was bobbing her hair. As Lowell walked to a seat to await his turn, he heard Claude say to the woman, "Why don't you let this fellow help you?" And he gestured with the scissors in Lowell's direction.

The woman turned to appraise the young man and, seemingly satisfied with what she saw, asked, "Can you run a job press?"

This is how Lowell, who was destined to become a teacher, became, instead, a newspaperman. The woman whose hair Claude was bobbing was co-owner of the weekly *Mitchell Tribune*. Lowell, who had learned to operate a job press and Linotype while working on the college newspaper, gave her his answer. He not only got the job, in 1945 he became the owner of the *Tribune* which he went on to operate for more than thirty years.

In the meantime, he tore up the Tampa contract and married the girl with whom he had fallen in love on the old Milwaukee. Many will remember her as their art teacher at Mitchell, Oolitic, Dive, Williams, East Oolitic, Huron, Shawswick schools. In her spare time she also helped the editor and publisher of the *Tribune* succeed in his newspaper venture.

Lowell came on the local newspaper scene while some of those who are remembered as "the old timers" in the business were still around: Charles Butler of the old *Bedford Times*, Fred Otis of the *Bedford Mail*, H. P. McCord, Preston G. Cox, and Camille Meno. And no one was ever more thankful for things turning out the way they did than Lowell.

"I've been more than fortunate," he told me during lunch that June day in 1986. "It's been an interesting life."

PINKSTON HILL

The grass is high and reddish-gold on the barren knoll. The early March wind is steady but not cold, the gift of a lingering winter's bright sun. The view for miles in every direction is one of rolling hills silhouetted against a distant horizon, their still naked trees stretching gaunt limbs to a high, ceramic blue sky. White-face cattle, shaggy in red winter coats, stand motionless amid the burnished stubble of last year's corn, and the mid-morning cackle of laying hens shatters the quiet. Except for the wind, that pushes and tugs at everything, and the demanding discordance of sound, it is peaceful. The very reason, perhaps, that old John Pinkston requested that his body be laid to rest at the very top of the knoll.

Within the confines of a rusted, now fallen-down wire fence clinging to leaning fenceposts, in a section that is some ten paces by ten paces, his is one of four graves in that tranquil place. A slight indentation to the left marks the final resting place of his wife, Sarah. To the left of her grave a fallen tombstone bears the inscription E. Pinkston, Feb. 5, 1876, July 9, 1907. Nothing more. To the left of that, standing erect in the pre-noon sunlight, is a small headstone with no markings whatsoever. John's tombstone is the white variety that usually marks the graves of Civil War soldiers.

The knoll is the highest point on Pinkston Hill, northwest of Fayetteville. I think it's north. If I were to stand at the crossroads in Fayetteville, at Larry Faubion's grocery store, I think I would point northwest to direct someone to it. After leaving Ott Flick and Emmerson Coyle in Harold Crane's barber shop, catty-corner from the grocery, I drove toward Silverville a ways and then turned north. However, when I got to Paul Peterson's place, which I thought was still north, Paul pointed to the Armstrong Station-Fayetteville Road, off to my right, which I thought should have been west, and said, "That's north."

If I don't know how I got to the knoll, I at least know how John Pinkston got there. While a young man he entered the Ohio River near LaGrange, Kentucky, and swam across to Indiana, eventually settling on what was to become Pinkston Hill. His lineage goes back to Pinkstone, England, and, according to the late Stella Lewis Pinkston Casada, of Bedford, is traced from there through North Carolina, Tennessee and Kentucky.

Mrs. Casada, who was the wife of Ollie Pinkston, until his death, was eighty-eight years old and lived at 601 Q Street when she gave me this information. She remembered John as "A fine looking old man" who stood as straight as a stake. Although he was unable to read or write, he was considered one of the best lawyers in these parts, having argued many cases before Monroe Circuit Court Judge J. B. Wilson. "He'd have the children read the (law) books to him, and he'd remember everything they read," Mrs. Casada remembered John's method of learning and preparing himself for trial.

One of his favorite readers was a girl named Alice Quackenbush. As Edith Pinkston Reath, 1813 15th

Street, and Gladys Pinkston Blackburn, 1818 14th Street, Bedford, were to relate to me, Alice was being courted by their father, Arthur Pinkston, at the time. And, as Alice would tell them in later years, after Sunday dinner at the home of Cassius and Alice Pinkston where John was living at the time, John would "Whip Alice away from the table" and have her read to him by the hour, and he'd commit every word to memory and repeat them after the reading sessions.

A witness to those sessions was Ollie, Arthur's brother, and "Uncle Phrates," whose grave is inscribed "E. (for Euphrates) Pinkston" up on that knoll on Pinkston Hill. Uncle Phrates lived in the house now occupied by Ott Flick. Still another reader was one of Arthur's six sisters, Mary Pinkston Todd, 2006 P Street, Bedford. "He'd make me read those law books," she remembered. "And when I got to a word I couldn't pronounce he'd say, 'Spell it,' and he'd listen to me spell it, then he'd pronounce it." When her brother, Ollie, was arrested for speeding through Oolitic in a buggy, John took his case and got him acquitted. Arthur not only had six sisters, he also had five brothers, and their mother was Alice Chaney Pinkston, Cassius's wife.

Besides Monroe County, John's legal talent also led him to courts in surrounding counties. On those trips, he often rode a "beautiful" black horse. He was a "very popular man," and there were times, when his clients lacked cash, that he was paid for his legal services in parcels of land. Some of that land was adjacent to that on which he had built his home and for that reason, and because of the several Pinkstons who lived there, it became known as Pinkston Hill.

Beyond Pinkston Hill the countryside continues its rolling beauty, and in time, the road leads to a T that crosses Indian Creek both to the left and to the right. Paul Petersen identified the T-road as the Silverville-

Owensburg Road, and it was he who directed me to the Old Bridge Church, on the banks of Indian Creek. It was there, in the creek, that Mary Todd and her twin sister, Cora Pinkston Faubion, and two of their other four sisters, Rose and Dallie, were baptized one Sunday.

Tryphena Pinkston Parks, Stella's daughter, remembered John as "Great Grandfather," while Mary Todd remembered him as "Grandfather." However he is remembered, one fact stands out, John Pinkston is legend, and what I have learned about him since my visit to that high, private burial ground has almost satisfied my curiosity about Pinkston Hill.

A COUNTRY REPORTER

Given the opportunity, few people, even she herself, could have summed up her lasting interest in newspapering as efficiently as did her boss, Sanford Deckard, late publisher of the *Shoals News*. "She was talking about quitting and retiring when she was sixty-five," Deckard recalled, "and I encouraged her to stay. She's eighty-one now."

Ruby Stiles, a stately woman with blue-gray hair, smiled that day, in early November, 1976, at the recollection of her near retirement sixteen years earlier. "I'm glad I didn't do it," she said. "I've enjoyed every minute of being a writer, even when people raise the devil with me."

A late bloomer in the business, Ruby was approaching the magical age of fifty when she began her newspaper career. She had taught school and had spent most of her life as a homemaker, wife and mother. She had more recently embarked on the happy years of grandmotherhood when Harry Strange, then owner of the *Shoals News*, asked her why she shouldn't consider writing for his paper.

"Well," Ruby recalled her answer, "you never did ask me." She remembered Harry's reply. "Well," he said jokingly, "I really didn't know if you could write."

Ruby said she retorted, "Well, Harry, I never did know if I could either." Laughing at the memory, she then said, "I never had, but I guessed I could, so I tried it and the more I did it the better I liked it."

Looking back, Ruby confessed a wish that she had started earlier. A tireless researcher, she wrote numerous historical pieces of early Martin County. She also authored many human interest stories. One of them, a story about the success in Florida of a Shoals resident, was published in *Fortune Magazine*. Her "Life of Dr. J. W. Strange" also received wide distribution, plus an Indiana Doctor of the Year Award for the physician. The most challenging stories she remembered were those surrounding the early arrival in Martin County of the gypsum industries.

"They were the most exciting stories," she recalled. "There were three companies here at one time. They came in here and wouldn't let us know what they were doing. What they were trying to do was lease or buy as much land for as little as possible. That was a good time then. In my stories I referred to gypsum as 'White Gold.' The mines have meant a lot to the economy of Martin County. The mines and Crane."

However exciting the coming of the gypsum companies might have been to her, Ruby's most popular work was her weekly column, "Headin' for the P.O." A collection of local names of local citizens and what they wore, said or did on their way to pick up their mail at the post office, it was unique. A hit with readers from its start, it gave them the kind of news about themselves that would have otherwise been impossible to put in a newspaper. Sometimes the column presented them with a good laugh at themselves.

"There was no home mail delivery here, and there still isn't," Ruby recounted. "We had trains back then, and you'd hear them coming through the middle of town, and all the trains brought mail. After every train, people would go to the post office. They'd wear whatever, and the grocer would roll his apron up over his belly, and go. And people stopped on the way and talked to one another about everything. And," she giggled, "I put as much of it as I could in the paper."

Her gaiety was short-lived with the onset of another thought. "We have only one delivery of mail a day now, by truck. And with all the traffic, nobody knows when it comes and when it goes. We had a good mail service back then. We don't have a good mail service anymore," she said sadly.

With the end of what she called a good mail service, readers of the *Shoals News* lost the pleasure of her weekly "Headin' for the P.O." Another column with the fixed head "This, That, and the Other," which took its place and ran on Page One of the paper was never, Ruby admitted, the zinger the other was.

As a successful small town newspaperwoman in those days, Ruby was rewarded at the rate of a nickel an inch for her writings. She was to earn more. "But," she added with straight-from-the-shoulder bluntness that would endear her to every self-respecting newspaper reporter, "you never make much money writing news."

She was sure that whatever it was that motivated her to become a newspaper reporter, was still motivating people in that direction. Of course, she pointed out, they refer to themselves as "journalists," now. Instead of being underpaid newspaper reporters, they are journalists trying to make it on underpaid newspaper reporter wages. And being such, they too were hopelessly caught up in the effects of what Ruby likened to the sting of a bee. "When the bee stings," she said, "you are stung."

"She's a real number one gal," publisher Deckard said of the stung Ruby. "She's done a real good job. She knows everybody, and she follows instructions very well. And she's loyal."

Until his death, Ruby's husband, A. B. "Bun" Stiles, was a merchant in Shoals. They were married in 1920, after he was discharged from the U.S. armed forces at the end of World War I, and after Ruby returned to Shoals from doing war work in Washington, D.C.

"I've been through four wars, not counting the Mexican War,"she said. "I remember the soldiers going through Shoals on trains to go to that one. They used to throw their names off on a piece of paper to the girls. One of my best friends got one, and she wrote to him. He was from Oil City, in Pennsylvania, and after the war he came back and they were married."

Although she was still working at this time, Ruby was not putting in the hours that she once did. Her reasoning for taking life easier was simply that, "After you get older, you get tireder." She had stopped driving her car, but she had not given up riding. There was a standing joke among her friends that Ruby would get into any car that stopped in front of her house. Ruby's answer to that was, "You bet. I go every time I get the chance."

We were seated comfortably in an enclosed porch that was Ruby's workshop. It was a cool place to work in summer and a whole lot cooler in winter. From where she sat, a sheet of copy paper was visible in the typewriter, a partially completed obituary Ruby was writing when my knock interrupted her.

"I hate to write them," she said raising her chin in the direction of the typewriter, more precisely the copy paper that was in it. "And especially if it is someone I know. I can see," she began recalling a related incident, "why the undertaker over here sold out and left. This is a small town and everybody knows everybody else. He said he got so he cried when anybody was brought in that he knew. And he was a young man, in his early thirties. He said he got to the place where he couldn't take it any longer. One day," she again nodded in the direction of the unfinished obit in the typewriter and, it seemed, deliberately avoiding the word death, she said, "I had eight of *them*. Most I knew personally. That's the thing that gets me most, when it's somebody I've been close to."

Ruby shrugged as though to shake off the subject and turned her recollections to happier stops along her long career: births, graduations, weddings, and the many other stories a reporter on a small town weekly is required to write. It was her opinion that the happiest assignments were school graduation stories. She had five grandchildren, and for a time they kept her on the run to their graduations.

Other than her marriage and her late husband and their son and her grandchildren, the best thing that ever happened to Ruby was "Mr. Deckard," who, after he bought out Harry Strange, "encouraged me to write, and he still does."

With age comes wisdom, and at eighty-one Ruby did not hesitate to admit to a fault that is universal among reporters, or staff writers, or journalists, or whatever those people who write news prefer to call themselves. "I get too long-winded, as you know we all do," she said.

And, presumably for that reason, a self-evaluation of her career, after I had asked her for it, was kept to a bare minimum. "I'm just a country reporter," she smiled knowingly, "and enjoying every minute of it."

NOAH

There was a time when folks there didn't have to consult the calendar to know that spring was on its way to Oolitic. Straw suitcases were the trusted harbingers. In the hands of newcomers, usually migrant Kentuckians and Tennesseans, they not only announced the beginning of the new season, but also the start of the year's stone quarrying season.

"They came up to work in the quarries that reopened every spring," said Noah Wagner. "And when the quarries shut down for the winter, they'd go back home. When we saw those straw suitcases, we knew that spring was near."

From his retirement farm home near Fayetteville, Noah recalled that Oolitic, then surrounded by numerous productive quarries, did not lack for people. "On a Saturday night, you had to get out into the street if you wanted to walk anyplace, there were that many people on the sidewalks," he said. "And Oolitic was a tough little place."

A liberal flow of liquid spirits made getting drunk an easy matter. That in turn promoted the usual Saturday night fights among celebrating quarry workers. Town Marshal "Pink" Bough was shot and killed on just such a night. It was Pink's death, and the riotous

170

Saturday nights, that produced the legendary John Gresham, perhaps the toughest marshal in the small limestone town's history. They also brought his successor, John Berger, who was perhaps the kindest marshal to wear a badge there. Both men are remembered for having administered law and order with equal success among the rabble.

Wagner's Garage was already a fixture in Oolitic. Noah had earlier met Euceba Sears at a tent meeting at Sentney School, in Possum Holler, and married her. They left Fayetteville and went to Terre Haute to live. Later, Noah and Euceba moved to Youngstown, Ohio. When they returned to Indiana in the early 1920s, Noah took over the garage in Oolitic, and they made their home there.

"We worked on more Model-T Fords than anything else," Noah said of the early days. "We'd grind the valves for two dollars, or overhaul the motor and the transmission for thirty-five dollars. Labor for a mechanic was eighty cents an hour."

He recalled that on one Kentucky Derby weekend he hand-pumped so many flat tires for passing motorists on the old Dixie Highway that he went out the following Monday and bought an air compressor for the garage. Two years after his November 1, 1923, opening of the garage, Noah's brother, Emory "Pug" Wagner, joined him in the business and remained there until 1940.

"We were born and raised in Indian Creek Township," Noah said. "In 1916 I graduated from Williams High School." He began naming his classmates, plucking each name from a flawless memory. "Leone Magerlein, Meta Dillman, Mabel Spreen, Homer Spreen, Harley Hall, Wendell McClung, Jane Williams and Mary Feltnor."

Sometime during his early school years, he saw his first automobile, a Saxon, which was owned and driven

171

by Dr. John McFarlin. Another was Sam McClung's Chandler, "Which," Noah said with a laugh, "was as long as from here," and he waved a hand in the direction of a window to indicate something out in the yard, "to the barn." Cars that came into his beginning years at the garage included Buick, Morman, Chalmers, Jewett, El Car, Reo Flying Cloud, Pierce Arrow, Packard and Jordan. But there weren't many of any of them around at a given time.

"There were times when I wouldn't take in any more than thirty-five cents a week," he said of the limited number of personally owned autos, and as a consequence, the difficulty to earn a livelihood. "But I had to either stay there or have no place to go," he said. "So I stayed."

Economic adversity brought about a period that Noah calls, the "Barter days." He and Euceba, by then the parents of two children, Harold and Sarah Jane, got their groceries from storekeepers Jimmy Hildum, Dell Watson, Poss Magnus and Grover Cudahy. Coal for heating the garage and the Wagner home came from John and Clint Robbins. "We traded work on their trucks and cars for our needs," Noah said. To earn extra money, Noah used to chauffeur Dr. Claude Dollens, a corpulent man who could not or would not operate an automobile, to the homes of his many patients around the county.

World War II changed all that. Wagner's Garage began seeing what Noah described as the "good times." Ten years later, he retired. "I bought this farm and went to work. It wasn't easy to stay here."

Noah recalled the pain of transition. Farming was challenging, but it was not the garage, it was not people and cars, it was not the smell of gasoline, oil and grease. "There were times," he recalled, "when I'd shut down the tractor, get into my pickup, drive to Eureka, and go south across Patton Hill to Oolitic.

172

And there I'd just have to look at, or walk through, the garage to get it out of my system. Then I'd be all right for a while."

While Noah put out corn and beans and wheat, and fattened cattle and hogs, Euceba, whom Noah still called "Honey" after sixty-five years of marriage, made a change in her life, too. Bill Smiley, who was trustee of Shawswick Township, was in need of office help. At age fifty Euceba applied for and got the job. She worked for Smiley until he left office, twenty-nine years later. Then she continued working for trustees Guy Weaver, Frank Johnson, and Marvin Dorsett. She also worked for county treasurers Daisy Black and Doris Asbell, and for assessor Harla East.

The Wagners lived in the house in which Euceba was born at the turn of the century. She was one of eleven children born to Frank and Arvada Freed Sears in the white frame dwelling which was built by her grandfather Peter Horn Sears. Noah's popularity did not end with auto mechanicking. Speak his name around old bird hunters, and some not so old, and they'll claim him as kith and kin. He had hunted birds since 1925 in Indiana, Kentucky, Mississippi and South Dakota. "Hunting quail," he avowed, "is the greatest of hunting sports." He remembered when the bag limit was sixteen, then twelve, then ten, "And, of course," he said sadly, "what it is now. Five." He added with a nostalgic shake of his head, "I remember when you could jump fifteen to twenty coveys in a day."

His hunting days came to an end one winter when he slipped on ice in his driveway and fractured his right hip. A surgically installed plastic socket and steel ball joint barely got him back on his feet when he fell out of the smokehouse and broke the other hip. Although he underwent two more surgical repairs, he was still unable to walk without the aid of a walker. It enabled him to putter around the house and yard.

"I'll tell you something," he said. "Broken hips will make an old man out of you."

He was still able to drive, and on good days he'd set out on a visiting trip. "I go to see old people," he said. "Elva Henderson at Springville, Ed Richards at Bedford, and some others." He smiled suddenly. "Folks say that I'm the biggest optimist they know. I'm eighty-two years old, I've got two broken hips, a thousand dollar bird dog and two brand new Remington shotguns."

Noah probably had the biggest sense of humor of anyone around, too.

HOLLACE SHERWOOD

In terms of violence, the most outstanding event to occur in Bryantsville probably was the shooting of the Rout brothers in 1904. Charles, thirty-four, and his brother, James, thirty-two, fell mortally wounded before the guns of John Tow and David Beasley.

The killings took place on an election day. "They were voting for a gravel road," remembered Mrs. John (Aunt Effie) Sherwood. At the time of my visit in November, 1974, she was perhaps the oldest resident of Lawrence County's Spice Valley Township.

On that same election day her nephew, Hollace Sherwood, was working in the garden at his home, and a little girl named Dorothy Bryant was visiting at Hollace's house. Each of them had heard the shots that ended two lives that day, but being young, and preoccupied as children can be, neither investigated the incident.

In that same year, a woman named Bertha died only hours after giving birth to an infant named Eva Lucille. Again Hollace and Dorothy were too young to take note. But eleven years later, they, and some seventy others who made up the small community, were aware of, and shocked by, the tragic death of Eva Lucille.

There is no way of learning from the pink granite headstone on Eva Lucille's grave the details that led up to that awful day. Besides her name, only the dates 1904-1915 appear thereon. But Dorothy remembered that Eva Lucille unexplainably dashed out of school that day. The girl ran to the Church of Christ Cemetery, knelt down at her mother's grave, and set herself ablaze.

"My brother had a new sweater, I remember," Dorothy recalled, "and they wrapped her in that."

A year after that tragedy, Dorothy graduated from Bryantsville High School. Five years earlier, Hollace had graduated from Mitchell High School. In order to attend classes there, he had made the daily twelve-mile round trip from Bryantsville by bicycle and horse and buggy. By this time, he had also chosen his lifelong profession – teaching.

After his graduation from Indiana University in 1916, he was assigned to King's Ridge School and was paid two dollars and nineteen cents a day. From there he went to Burton School where he taught for one year. A stint at Bryantsville High School the next year was followed by a year at Mitchell High School. As principal, and with a salary of fourteen hundred dollars a year, he opened the doors to the then new Burris Elementary School, at Mitchell, the next school term. He remained until his retirement in 1957.

Dorothy received her degree in 1922, and on June 2 of that year she and Hollace were married. When fall came, she began her brief teaching career at Tinsley Ridge School, east of Merry's Station on U.S. 50, some dozen miles west of Bedford. "I rode horseback to school," she said of the three-mile daily trip to Tinsley Ridge. "Not a sidesaddle, but a regular saddle." She recalled that she wore skirts which weren't long, but longer than they are today," while riding, and, "There wasn't anybody much along the road and not too many houses. When it was cold, I rode in a cart."

Dorothy also had taught at Bryantsville, but her last year was spent at Williams, "Over the river." It was after that school year that she and Hollace began raising a family. There were born to them Hollace Daniel, John Robert, James Noble, and Ralph Edward. All but one were born in the house that had been Hollace's home from the moment he was born, and Dorothy's since that day in June, 1922, when he brought her home as his bride.

A two story white frame house of more than a dozen rooms, there stretched invitingly across its front a handsome railed porch. Immediately above that was another porch accessible only from the second floor. There were a variety of trees surrounding the house. Some, which rose from large circular boles, were planted by Hollace and Dorothy the summer of their marriage. It struck me as a house of houses. In my imagination I could hear the sounds of life and living emanating from its many rooms. In the silence of imagined night I could hear the haunting whistles of freight trains plodding on railroad tracks three miles distant. Hollace's four brothers were also born there. And it was in that house that an eighty-two year old Hollace smiled and said of the many Sherwood family members in Lawrence County, "I think we all belong to the same breed of cats."

Of his days at Burris, he recalled how he instituted Friday morning chapel services at which he taught the Sunday School lesson of the week. Noting the effect his voluntary action had on pupils, Gladys (Stevens) Isom, of Mitchell, once said, "You could always tell at Sunday School which kids went to Burris School."

"Teachers commanded respect in those days," Hollace said. "And parents instructed their children that 'if you get a lickin' at school, you'll get another one when you get home.' "

Bryantsville was platted May 28, 1835, by Henry Connelly, and named Paris. Susan Adelle Connelly,

Hollace's mother, was a descendant of Henry Connelly, and she married Daniel Webster Sherwood. How and why Paris became Bryantsville neither Hollace nor Dorothy could say. Judging from evidence appearing on tombstones in the churchyard cemetery, there was a preponderance of Bryants there, including Dorothy's father, Oliver Cromwell Bryant. Whatever it was, or may have been, Bryantsville by this time was a memory. If it existed physically, it was in the presence of the church, or a portion of the school wall whose crumbling bricks were visible on a high bank. Perhaps it lived in the presence of the Sherwood home, and others like it.

During his assignment to King's Ridge, Hollace tutored more than fifty children enrolled in the one room school house. "I had room for them only because they were never all there on the same day," he recalled, "and because two children sat at each desk."

Trustees were overseers of the schools. The days prior to fall school opening saw them contracting to hire teachers and to have school woodsheds filled. It was a trustee in 1955 who put an end to Friday chapel services at Burris School by relieving Hollace of his principalship. "I want to restore education to what it was when my mother was a school teacher," Hollace quoted the trustee who fired him. Two years later, Hollace took retirement.

For a growing boy in rural Spice Valley Township, the arrival of the weekly newspaper was an exciting event. "I remember reading about the Spanish American War, and Roosevelt and his Rough Riders," Hollace's eyes brightened. "And I remember Dewey going to Manila, and the *Oregon* making its way around Cape Horn to join the fleet . . . "

Although he was college educated, he maintained the ways of the rural area in which he had grown up. One of these was the ability to use a gun. Having

178

become a member of the National Guard while attending IU (it was not the ROTC then) he considered himself capable of serving with his company when it was federalized and committed to the bloody pursuit of Pancho Villa.

"They wouldn't have me," Hollace recalled. "I only stood five-feet-two and weighed about a hundred pounds, and someone said, 'Why he won't be able to stand up under a pack'."

His company captain took issue with this decision, declaring that, "He's the only man in this whole company who knows which end of a gun the bullet comes out of."

He remembered that IU professor Kenneth Williams was the lieutenant of his college National Guard company. When he tried to volunteer for service in World War I, Hollace, again because of his size, was turned down. He went home then to grow and harvest wheat with his father and brothers on the more than five hundred acre Sherwood farm.

Hollace and his wife had stored up many memories of Bryantsville and what life was like in and near that community. As the arrival of the weekly newspaper was an occasion for excitement, so were the infrequent trips the family made to Bedford. "Sometimes we'd spend the better part of a day going there in a farm wagon, depending on the weather conditions," Hollace said.

The ten-mile ride to Robertson's Feed Mill at the corner of 17th and L streets was made in less than three hours. "We took our wheat and corn there to be ground," he recounted, "and we bought our staples to bring home. We bought sugar by the barrel — five hundred and eighty pounds to the barrel — at two and three cents a pound. I remember how we used to roll it in through the door and into the pantry. Father would take the head of the barrel out very carefully

179

and put a handle on it so you could lift it up and dip the sugar out."

Dorothy remembered her grandfather, Dr. Addison Bare, practicing medicine and delivering babies. "He rode a buggy all over this part of the country," she recalled. She also remembered the winter drowning of a small boy in a pond near the church. "We were never allowed to go near the pond in winter," she said. "There was one part of it that never froze over, or it froze over only in a thin layer of ice and not thick enough to hold anyone."

Midway between Hollace and Dorothy's house, and Aunt Effie's, the church, with its tall spire, rose from a windswept knoll. Inside, a series of thick beams lined an expanse of cathedral ceiling. Hexagonal light fixtures three feet long were suspended from gilded chains measuring four feet in length. There were no benches or traditional pews. Theater-type seats filled the sanctuary. In the two aisles that ran between the main seating area and those on the sides of the large room, wine carpeting led to the altar. Wine carpeting also led down a basement stairway at the foot of which were Sunday School rooms, two restrooms and a kitchen.

Four months after this visit, I returned to Bryantsville and the Church of Christ Cemetery. From where I stood, the snowy spring that had preceded me there was visible in the surrounding hills and woodlands. It was peaceful and still. Yet, there was a noticeable disruption. A new grave was there. That of Hollace Sherwood. It brought memories of the previous November. The day he and Dorothy and I sat at a table in the Sherwood kitchen. He was a short, slight man – almost fragile, I found myself thinking. Yet, it struck me that if Hollace Sherwood *wasn't* something, it was fragile. He was a very strong man. His small frame had stood straight and tirelessly under an assumed burden few men of his time would have dared take upon themselves.

I remembered the account of his dismissal from the principalship of Burris for daring to teach from the Bible in a public school, the words of the trustee who fired him, and how Dorothy had retorted, "The devil got after him, that's what that was all about." I remembered Hollace saying that as a parent and teacher he was a disciplinarian with Victorian influences, but that he first was Hollace Sherwood, the man. "Think the best of every child," was his conviction, "and he will strive to measure up to it." I remembered that near to the close of my interview with him that November day I had asked, "If you were to look deep within yourself, your past, what kind of man would you say you are?"

Hollace was thoughtful for a few moments. Then with the hint of a smile brightening his face, he said, "Oh, I'd say I'm a man just waiting for the Lord to come."

I knew then that whatever it was men are supposed to do on this earth, Hollace had done it, and that he'd done it to the very best of his ability. I knew, too, that other springs would come to Bryantsville, but there would be an emptiness in them.

COOL FRAN

Chuck Ross had always said that if a holdup man ever took on his store at Cunot, his wife, Fran, would blow her cool. "She just wouldn't be able to take it," Chuck would tell his friends and customers. "Not Fran. Never," he'd say.

Luckily, when one did, Fran was at home and not in the store. "Thank goodness," intoned Chuck. "A panicky woman around at the time of an armed robbery cannot be construed as an asset."

Barbara Grant was there. A former worker in the fingerprint section at Indiana State Police headquarters in Indianapolis, she had moved to that remote northern corner of Owen County and taken a job at Chuck's Corner Grocery. She was seated at one checkout counter and Chuck was seated at the other, enjoying the usual lull before evening closing at seven-thirty. Barbara was chit-chatting with a customer, and the woman's daughter, while Chuck had busied himself with pre-closing tasks.

A man walked in, meandered around the small country store, then left without making a purchase. In a minute or two he returned. Approaching Chuck, he pointed a gun at him and, nodding in the direction of the rear of the store, growled, "Get back there."

"You're kidding," Chuck smiled. "This is some kind of joke, isn't it?"

182

The armed man jabbed the gun at the six-foot-two, three hundred and forty pound store owner and said threateningly, "No, I'm not kidding. This is not a joke."

Barbara, who was only feet away was oblivious to the action. So were her friends with whom she continued to chit-chat. And then the armed man pointed the gun at the mother and daughter and ordered them to follow Chuck, and told Barbara, "You stay there."

At the rear of the store, the trio was ordered to lie face down on the floor, with the warning, "Stay there unless you want to get hurt." Then the holdup man returned to Barbara. "I'll take the money," he pointed the gun at her and then to her cash register. "Open it up."

Barbara was stunned by the sudden turn of events – a holdup man, the ugly gun in the robber's hand, Chuck and her friends lying on the floor, the demand for money – but she kept her cool. She pushed the lever that opened the cash drawer of the big register. It failed to function. Impossible! She hit it again! She punched it! All to no avail. She was on the verge of panic when suddenly she thought to tilt her head ceilingward and pray. "Please, God," she petitioned, "help me get this thing open." In response to her next punch on the lever there was a welcome miracle. Accompanied by a rattle and a ring-a-ding, the reluctant cash drawer popped outward. Barbara's brief dilemma apparently had shaken the holdup man; he took only what was in the drawer of her cash register and fled to a waiting car driven by a companion.

The incident brought about a lasting change at Chuck's Corner Grocery. "We've been closing at 6 o'clock ever since," Chuck explained. But the new hours were no barrier to the subsequent recountings of what happened there that evening. And almost every time he related the incident Chuck would say, "It's a good thing Fran wasn't there. She'd have blown her cool. She'd have been so nervous she'd've got us all killed."

The following Christmas season, Chuck and Fran returned late from a shopping trip. In the van he was driving were Fran's new kitchen cabinets. In the old Buick she was driving were numerous gifts the couple had purchased for family and friends. In both vehicles there was that good spirit of Christmas. As Chuck wheeled the van into the store parking lot the headlights swept the white building with a sudden golden light. The sight filled Chuck with a sense of relief. It was good to be home. He went to the door with keys in hand and stopped short at the sight of a broken window. He suggested that Fran wait in the car until he checked out the store. Although he saw evidence of a break-in, he was unable to find anyone. He called to Fran, "He's gone." And he motioned for her to come in.

Who was gone? Actually, no one. When Fran joined Chuck in the store, and he was dialing the sheriff to report the break-in, an intruder suddenly appeared. A stranger, he was clad in coveralls. "Hang up the phone," he ordered Chuck, "or I'll blow your head off."

Remembering that he slammed down the phone as he was bidden, the giant store owner added, "He was just a young slip of a thing and I could have taken him easily. But he said he had a .357 magnum in his pocket. He said, 'Don't try anything,' and he told me and Fran about the gun and he said, 'I know how to use it, too.' So I didn't try anything."

The youthful bandit demanded money. Since there was none in either of the cash registers in the store, he took nine dollars from Chuck's wallet and thirty-five dollars from Fran's purse. He also took two packages of sliced ham from the meat section of the store. As he prepared to leave, he said to Chuck, "Give me the keys to the car."

Fran, knowing that her husband had the keys to the van suddenly blurted, "Don't you take the van. My cabinets are in there." And she offered the holdup man her keys to the Buick. "You're going to drive," he advised Fran. "Get out there behind the wheel."

Fran did as she was ordered. Her passenger directed her to another Cunot business place. And while he

184

forced his way into that store and brazenly robbed it, Fran was his captive companion and driver of his get-away car. A few miles later, the young thief pointed to a desolate stretch of road and told Fran to stop. "Get out of the car," he threatened her with hand in pocket.

"You can't put me out here in the dark of night like this without a light," Fran argued. "Give me a flashlight, right there, see?" She pointed to a flashlight in the car. "I might need it." The robber argued back, saying he himself might need it. "You surely won't need two of them, and there are two of them in the car," Fran shot back. The youth looked at her incredulously. He glanced quickly around the car. He saw the reflection of the dome light off a second flashlight. "Here," he said giving Fran a flashlight, and he put the car in gear.

"Wait," Fran called. "Give me my Christmas packages. You surely won't need them."

"Take them! Take them!" the frenzied young robber shouted at her, pushing and shoving the packages toward her.

Fran took her time, not missing a single package. When she had them all, the car sped away. With the aid of the salvaged flashlight, she concealed the packages in a ditch. She then walked until she arrived at a house where she asked to use the phone.

When Chuck, who was beside himself with worry about his wife, finally put down the store telephone (after calling the sheriff, state police, CB clubs, friends and whoever else he thought might help rescue Fran), his wife got through to him.

"Come and get me," she said over the telephone.

Later, from a seat on a chair in the store, from which a relieved Fran detailed her experience to her husband, police, CB club members and friends who'd rushed to Cunot in response to Chuck's calls, a cascade of tears suddenly fell from her eyes. Looking up at Chuck she sobbed, "See, I didn't lose my cool."

THAT LOVIN' FEELIN'

Jim Polk picked his way back through the years humming bits of Faron Young's "Sweet Dreams," Hank Williams' "Your Cheatin' Heart," Glenn Miller's "In The Mood," and Ray Price's "Crazy Arms."

"Sweet dreams of you –" he repeated a few words of Young's popular song, "things I know can never come true . . ."

There were more songs he wanted to sing, but Jim shook his head. "The words just won't come to mind this minute," he apologized.

Jim's son, Scott, laughed. "Go home and get your guitar, Dad," he said.

Father and son laughed. They both knew that with a guitar in his hands, songs, old and new, would come back to Jim with no problem. Tough luck. Jim was unable to cut hair and play a guitar at the same time, and this was hair-cutting time in his barber shop in Bedford.

Jim was a boy of ten when he began playing guitar with his father, fiddler Edgar Polk. "He played both for personal pleasure and for square dances," Jim recalled how he got started playing the guitar. "Dad showed me a few chords, enough to back him up. From then on, I listened and watched."

He launched on a recollection of other musicians whom he had watched, to whom he had listened, with whom he had played. Les Grisson; Dale Spinks, a popular lead guitarist in the Bedford-Lawrence County area; J. R. White, of Paoli, whose voice and guitar were once popular in south central Indiana; Harold Fullen, a guitarist and singer; Harold Fisher, who was perhaps the greatest self-taught musician to emerge at that time from that same area; Bud Isaacs, who began his musical career with Fisher and later moved on to Nashville, Tennessee, and of whom Jim said, "was, and still is, one tough steel guitarist."

There were others: Jim Ramage, Dave Swartz, Dick Green, Alan McKenzie and, said Jim, "The slickest guitar man ever to come out of Bedford, Billy Fender. He's retired from the Navy now and is living in Hollywood, California."

Billy's name framed the era in which his name and the names of many more musicians were popular on the Bedford music scene. It was the golden era of the town's honky-tonks, a period when they ran wide open and their back doors saw more foot traffic than their front doors. Torphy's, The Wicket, Lockhart's, The Grande Grille. They operated with impunity within a stone's throw of the Bedford police station, a block and a half from the Lawrence County jail and a short walk from some of the town's churches.

None heard as dice galloped the long, green back room courses carrying the hopes of crap shooters. Nor did they hear the shuddering of Blackjack tables under the balled fists of deluded losers. The smacking, clinking, pounding of dice-filled leather cups at Twenty-Six tables also went unheard, as did the clinking of ice cubes in glasses of illegally sold booze.

A part of the scene and offering a change of pace were The Friendly, Kenny's, The City, The Old Colonial and Brown's. There were also the Coke and ice set-up joints for after closing revelry: Tarry Park and the Green Lantern, both on the Old Dixie Highway south of Bedford. Those who set themselves above honky-tonking, the open gambling, the setup joints, led the full life behind the locked doors of the private fraternal clubs.

The town and county ran wide open and there arose from the din the loud but pure sounds of hillbilly music as played by most of the above. Jim Polk, a handsome young man in those days, always smartly dressed, was one of them. They were members of make-up combos, bands – as they referred to their groups – and they played all the "hot" spots. "There were times when we played just for drinks," Jim smiled at the memory. "We usually came away feeling pretty good."

That memory reminded him of a night when Earl Chandler, Dan Gullett, and Orville Pruett played at Spring Mill State Park and got five dollars, and no drinks. Another night they played at French Lick Springs Hotel and they received fifteen dollars and all they could drink. Some who played in the early bands were too young to be in barrooms, taverns and joints. But state excise police rarely checked.

Booze aside, the young and older musicians had a common goal. Success: making the Nashville scene. In that never-ending quest they switched from one band to another, hoping to find the right combination. Daytime found them living different lives. Jim, beginning in 1937, spent his days standing at a barber chair. At fifty-three, he was still a barber, a profession he shared with his son, Scott, in the shop at Bedford. At this time, in 1975, he was still a barber of the old school, a hair-cutter, while Scott, following later trends, was "A hair stylist specialist."

They shared more. They were members of a musical group billed as "Jim Polk and the Good Times." Besides Jim, who was boss man and bass guitarist, and Scott, the rhythm guitarist, the group included

188

Denny Roberts, lead guitarist, Gary Shaw, drummer, and Steve Shaw, vocalist.

The term "hillbilly music" long ago faded from the world of music and "country western," "country," and "country rock," had come into being. Such was the make-up of The Good Times group that those categories were separated by generations. But there was no problem. Age and time were easily overcome by understanding and cooperation. "They teach me country rock, I teach them country and country western," Jim explained.

But even cooperation and understanding had their limits. The hillbilly music player of long ago found that standing at a barber chair his days had become longer, and that nights of guitar-picking had begun to lengthen. "These young ones," Jim said of the other members of his group, "can go all week long, working every day and playing every night. But I'm getting too old."

Engagements usually were arranged for Friday and Saturday nights. While Sunday was always a day of rest for the old man, Saturday, traditionally a busy day for barbers, was for him the longest day of the week. So was Saturday night playing his guitar in some barroom the longest night. Since the shop was open six days, there were no rejuvenating weekday naps for him. Despite his limitations, Jim determined to keep going. "Playing," he confided, "is a fun thing for me, and it has been all my life."

As the "fun thing" was passed to him by his father, so had Jim passed it on to his son, Scott. "When he was seven," Jim said, "I bought him a guitar and told him, 'Now hit the road.' " It was meant as a joke. But that road led Scott to his father and The Good Times, and an enviable father-son relationship.

Still, for Jim, there was more. The pleasure of recalling the good times, and, to borrow from a lyrist, "That lovin', feelin' " he had for his guitar.

DENNIS PRUETT

George Edwards was still a young man when he bought Dennis Pruett's stock of groceries in 1966. George had visions of a long future as a Huron businessman. Dennis, considerably older than George, and glad to end his tenure as a businessman there, was hoping for a few years of retirement.

"I'd been in the store business thirty-three years and lost fifteen thousand dollars," Dennis reminisced on a bright day in February, 1976. "And I was happy to get out."

George's life had been brief. After his death the large store he'd hoped would provide him with a future was sold to brothers Dwight and Dwain Allbright, two young men. They were not the first Allbrights to operate a general store in Huron. Homer Allbright once operated a very large one there, and he also ran five huckster routes out of the once prosperous town.

That's when Dennis got his feet wet in the store business. He and Menlo Tackett worked one of the huckster routes together. In one day they'd travel as far as Powell Valley, and Abbeydell. They'd return in the evening with as many as a hundred and twenty-five cases of eggs, and coops full of live chickens they'd taken in trade for staples and groceries.

Dennis and Menlo formed a friendship that would last a lifetime. Such attachments were not unusual in the life of Huron. When Howard Terry marked his ninetieth birthday anniversary, more than a hundred well-wishers stopped at his home. Many of them had been lifelong friends. They also provided Mr. Terry with a money tree, which made him richer by a couple hundred dollars.

Dennis wasn't always in the grocery store business. He was a brick mason once, and in the 1920s and early 1930s he helped build many residences in Bloomington. The largest building he ever helped to construct there was the J. C. Penney Co. store, at North College Avenue and Courthouse Square. The Great Depression sent him back to Huron, where he found the grocery business attractive enough to begin devoting the rest of his working days to it.

"I made a living," he said of his effort, "and I suppose that's about all a fellow can ask."

Long before that, before he left Huron to work in Bloomington, Dennis worked for Carpenter Body Works in Mitchell. "We built horse-drawn school buses in those days. We built eighteen a year, and worked eleven hours a day for thirty cents an hour. I was offered a dollar an hour in Bloomington, and that's why I went there," he recalled.

Despite his losses, he took pleasure in remembering the gain of one rural resident. "He bought forty acres for four dollars, and planted thirty-six thousand government trees on it that didn't cost him anything. He lived to see them trees grow up, and to sell them for a dollar and fifty-cents a tree."

Much of the fifteen thousand dollar loss Dennis sustained was in family grocery bills of two hundred and three hundred dollars each.

"Somebody'd get sick, or maybe they'd be out of work, or they'd have a death, and they'd ask you to carry them," he recounted. "How could you say no? So you'd carry them, and then they'd run up a big bill. Those who intended to pay their grocery bills, paid them. Those who didn't intend to pay, didn't. I remember one man who owed me nine hundred dollars. He went to the bank and borrowed the money to pay me. Afterward, he paid the bank twenty-nine dollars a month, until he paid them off. He was a good man. Just the other day a fellow came in here to the house and paid me ten dollars on his bill. That left him three hundred and ninety-eight dollars. It was four hundred and ninety-five dollars in 1966, when George bought me out. He's the only one paying, of all them owing me. I gave him the receipt book and told him to take it home. I'll come as near getting it with him keeping the book as me keeping it."

He paused and held up a hand. "You know," he shook his head thoughtfully, "there was a family here that had seventeen or eighteen children, and they traded with me and paid me everything they owed. They don't owe me a dime. Now you'd think that if a family that size could pay, anybody could, now wouldn't you?"

Dennis spent very little time counting the money he was certain he'd never collect. After his wife, Ruby, retired from teaching school forty-five years, she became a speech therapist. Her work took her to area schools, hospitals and convalescent centers, and Dennis was pleased about that. They shared a small white house at the end of Railroad Avenue, near the B&O railbed, the joys of their five grandchildren, and their daughter, Margaret Dunbar.

He also had a story or two up his sleeve. One concerned a hobo. He recalled a day in the store when he and Menlo saw the man walking up the B&O tracks.

"They were always stopping in the store wanting something to eat," he began. "There were a lot of them in those days, and, if you fed one, he'd tell the rest of them, and here they'd come. Well, sir, this fellow was coming up the railroad, and I told Menlo, 'Get the guns.' We stuck one gun out from behind some ten-pound sugar sacks, and the others out from barrels and shelves. And when the fellow came through the door I reached up and got the end of the string we always had overhead to tie packages with, and I said, 'Stop right there.' He stopped and looked at me, and I said, 'See all those guns?' He looked around at all those guns pointing toward the door where he was, and you could tell he got scared. I said, 'All I have to do is pull this string and all those guns will go off at the same time and blow you right out of here.' Oh, that scared him. I said to him, then, 'I'm going to feed you, but you be careful what you tell anyone about me feeding you. And when you leave, don't look back, and don't come back through that door, or I'll pull this string.' He ate, and he got, and we never saw him again."

There were five stores in Huron, then: Elmore & Pitman's; George Conley's; Ben Ratliff's; Everett Sorrells's, and Dennis's. There was another, but it was a small place: Howard Terrell's. He always kept a big pot of vegetable soup on a stove. A large bowl with oyster crackers cost a dime, and a hunk of pickled baloney to go with it cost a nickel.

ANTIQUE ALLEY

Spring days and nights I liked to lounge around Nashville, taking notes on all I'd see and hear. It was my time there, when unharried shop owners and natives were inclined to sit around and chew the fat. That old feeling had a good grip on me one day while I was down in Antique Alley. Ralph Yoder, an angular jawed, elderly native was there. As was Alice Weaver, a retired registered nurse and then co-owner of the near-by lucrative Old Ferguson House. We were seated together on benches and Ralph was recalling something banker Jimmy Tilton had said in connection with the old place. That was years earlier, right after Allie Ferguson and her sister, Molly, had done with the old boarding house they'd operated for so long.

"The whole place was for sale for fourteen hundred dollars," Ralph said loudly. Ralph always spoke up that way because he was hard of hearing. "And when Jimmy heard about it, he says to me, 'That's a good buy, Ralph – for somebody that wants it.' "

As proprietors of the place at this time, Alice and her husband, Dick, were sitting on a small fortune; "a gold mine," was how many of their competitors put it. An unpainted, shabby, junk-filled two story affair, the Old Ferguson House had become one of the more popular tourist attractions in Nashville and Brown County. And Ralph had not only passed it up for a pithy fourteen hundred dollars several years earlier, he had also lived long enough to regret his error.

"I never made any money till I quit working when I was twenty-five years old and went to selling real estate," he said, adding that while he did miss buying the Ferguson place, he at least did have a happy experience in it when it was a boarding house. "It was about 1901," he began his recollection of it. "My teacher from up on Owl Creek was staying there. I had to come to town, and my mother said, 'Why don't you stop and say hello to him. He might just give you a treat.' And I did. And he did. He gave me three sticks of candy." Ralph swallowed a couple of times, rubbed a hand across his mouth, and he added, "I can remember that so well, but I can't remember what happened yesterday."

Having noticed the same problem developing with my own memory, I offered a sympathetic rejoinder. "Tell me about it, Ralph," I said. And he replied, "What did you say?" And Alice growled, "Ralph, for goodness sake! When are you going to get a hearing aid?" And Ralph said to Alice, "What did you say?"

Don't think I'm poking fun at Ralph. I'm not. Besides being likeable, Ralph could probably have bought me for what I thought I was worth at that time and sold me at market value and never felt the pinch. In addition to all that, he said such things as "gee-whiz," and "ahdreckon," and I never poke fun at Hoosiers who say such things as that.

It so happened that just then a jogger wearing brightly colored sweats bounced through Antique Alley and passed near us. Ralph watched the runner for a moment and then turning to us he declared just under a shout, "You see them a-going jog, jog, jog, jog, jog, and jog." He bounced in his seat and worked his forearms to imitate a runner, huffing and puffing as he spoke. "Why that's silly," he went on. "They say it'll make you live a long time. Pshaw! I never did jog a step in my life and I'm eighty-seven years old. Jogging," he suddenly groaned in complete denial of the benefits of exercise, "won't keep you alive." He turned his attention directly to Alice. "Did you ever do any thing silly like that, Alice? Did you ever jog?" he asked.

Alice looked at him thoughtfully for a few seconds then retorted, "No, I never did, Ralph. But when I was a nurse working in the hospital and I was carrying a full bedpan I did walk a little fast."

It was obvious Ralph hadn't heard. He wrinkled his brow in perplexity and shouted, "What? What did you say?" And Alice again cried out to him, "Ralph, for goodness sake! Why don't you buy a hearing aid!"

The message got through the bone in Ralph's ears that time. "Hearing aid!" he exploded. He dug his wallet out of a pocket, slipped some two dollar bills out of the way and brought forth from its depths a folded white paper. "I got this piece of paper just for people like you to read," he shoved the paper under Alice's nose. "See there, where it says hearing aids ain't for everyone?"

Alice pushed his hand away and took the paper. It was a hearing aid advertisement. Sure enough, one line in the ad did note that hearing aids are not for everyone. And Ralph, without ever having submitted to an examination, saw himself as one of those persons who could not benefit from such an acquisition. More characteristically, he stressed the economy of his kind of thinking. Returning the ad to his wallet he began fidgeting to leave us.

I asked, "Where are you going, Ralph?"

"Around," he replied with a wide fling of a hand that was meant to take in all of Nashville. "You've got to go someplace. I'm going around."

I looked after him, thinking I was sorry to see him go, and in so doing I missed hearing some of what Alice was saying about Brown County characters. When I finally got tuned in to her she was talking about an incident of a few years earlier that involved a Nashville doctor.

"He had put up a big sign over his office that read, 'Proctologist.'" she said. "And the next time I saw him I said, 'Hey, Doc, I saw your new sign. I didn't know that you told fortunes.'

"Well, he knew I was an RN and he looked at me in the strangest way and he said, 'By golly, if you don't know what that means, I'm taking that sign down.' "

Alice and her husband, Dick, acquired the Ferguson place in 1958. In addition to a couple of floors of antiques, oddities and glassware, and several outside stalls filled with more antiques, the place included a huge family of cats. There were long-haired and short-haired cats, cats with tails and cats without tails, and cats of various colors. Among them there was usually a litter of kittens, and among those there were always two kittens that Alice could never seem to find.

"I don't count them," she replied when I asked her one day the numerical size of the feline collection. "I just feed them, and look for those two kittens."

That's how she came to be in Antique Alley so early in the week when I found her with Ralph. Long before business hours, she'd driven from her home in the country to feed her cats. She did the same every morning in the spring, summer, fall and winter. Even when she had to wade snow "up to here," she made a cutting motion with the heel of a hand midway on a thigh.

Alice had appeared in my column several times, usually after she had spoken out for the benefit of the Nashville business community. Her criticism of the continued failure of town fathers to provide adequate parking and restroom facilities for those thousands of tourists who annually poured their money into the town's cash registers had always been fascinatingly eloquent. The long, cold winter had not cooled her. And after Ralph had gone his way, she took the opportunity to comment on one of the goals of the Brown County Recreation and Industrial Development Council which read: "To encourage and promote the tourist business in Brown County."

She said: "I'm all for it. But if you drive into Nashville with a full bladder and there is no place to park, you say to hell with it and drive on — till you get to the next bush, anyway. Before we send out invitations to the party, we ought to get ready for the guests.

197

And getting ready means the basics – parking and restrooms. And restrooms include toilet facilities for the handicapped."

Alice and Dick did very little to improve the appearance of the Old Ferguson House. Apparently the old look is what tourists liked about the place. It was stocked with all manner of antiques, some so expensive she often refused to let children come inside, fearing they might damage valuable merchandise. She was not mean about it, just adamantly firm. But she had a withering way with words and, if it was necessary, she could get rough about it, too. Because she was so outspoken and willing to be quoted in a column, I usually made the Old Ferguson House a stop when I was in Nashville. A week or so after I had written a Sunday column about a human skeleton she kept on the second floor of the Old Ferguson House I stopped in to see Alice. When she saw me she went on the attack.

"What the hell did you try to do to me Sunday?" she demanded. "When we got here people were lined up outside all the way to the corner, and around the corner all the way up Van Buren Street. We had people lined up all day, going upstairs to see that damn skeleton. We had one hell of a lot of people go through this place. But," she finally disclosed what I presumed was the reason for her anger, "we didn't sell anything. Not a damn thing!"

Despite that no sale Sunday, the rumor persisted that she and Dick made plenty of money there. And, to their credit, they tried to put some of it back into Nashville. Alice consistently put up the good fight for improvements in the tourist town, with little success. She did not live to see it, but additional parking and public restrooms at last became a reality there.

If you enjoy Nashville in the spring of the year – as I enjoy it – or at any other season of the year, restrooms are no longer an insurmountable problem, if you can endure the long lines of waiting tourists. If you can't, well, as Alice might have suggested, look for a bush.